Michael Frayn

Sweet Dreams

FLAMINGO

Published by Fontana Paperbacks

First published by
William Collins Sons & Co. Ltd 1973
First issued in Fontana Paperbacks 1979
This Flamingo edition first published March 1986

Flamingo is an imprint of
Fontana Paperbacks, a division of
the Collins Publishing Group
8 Grafton Street, London W1X 3LA

Made and printed in Great Britain by
William Collins Sons & Co. Ltd, Glasgow

A man sits in his car at the traffic-lights, waiting for them to go green.

He is thirty-seven years old, with high forehead, and thin hair that stands on end in the slightest breeze. His eyes are a little protuberant, and his lips are set in a faint smile, so that as he leans forward against the wheel, gazing straight ahead through the windscreen, he seems to be waiting for the green light with eagerness.

In fact the light has been green for some time already.

Howard Baker (this is his name) is sitting in front of a green light waiting for a green light because he is thinking. He is wondering:

– whether he is adequately insured;

– whether it's Hornsey Lane he is about to enter on the other side of Highgate Hill, or whether he has confused Highgate Hill with Highgate West Hill once again;

– whether life might really be coming to an end, as ecologists say;

– whether he should kiss Rose, the wife of the man he is on his way to see, when she opens the front door to him;

– whether, conceptually, it would be helpful to try regarding the house as an extension of the car, rather than the other way about, and experimenting with an internal trim based upon black simulated leather, with built-in ashtrays;

– whether he will be invited to lunch with Rose and Phil, and if not, whether to get a sandwich in a pub, or go straight back to the office, send out for sandwiches, and catch up on the plans for the Manchester Marina scheme; and if so, whether to order egg and tomato sandwiches, or cheese and chutney, or some of each;

– whether the girl standing on the opposite side of Highgate Hill (or Highgate West Hill) with the long dark hair blowing forwards over her shoulders will turn so that he can see her face; and if so whether the face will be the revelation that the long dark hair promises; and what a face would have to be *like* to be the revelation that one always expects . . .

Another car pulls up behind him, and hoots discreetly – pup-pup. He does not hear it.

The lights go yellow.

The girl is just about to turn. She is gazing up Highgate Hill (or Highgate West Hill), waiting for someone. At any moment she will turn round and check that her friend is not coming from the opposite direction.

The lights go red.

Howard Baker now recalls an unanalysed sound waiting in his memory for attention – a pup-pup, a sound of hooting. He looks quickly in his mirror, and sees the head of the man in the car behind move from side to side with sardonic patience. Smiling foolishly, he puts the car into gear, and violently accelerates away, taking one last look at the girl, just in case she turns.

And she does. She turns to look at *him*. Her face is astonished – blank with astonishment. An attractive face, with dark eyes and dark eyebrows, but no revelation. Just amazed, with the mouth a little open, as if preparing to formulate some cry.

So that's one thing settled. The problem of lunch he doesn't resolve, nor whether to kiss Rose, nor the question of internal trim in public housing. But he does find out whether it's Hornsey Lane on the other side of Highgate Hill (or Highgate West Hill).

It's not. It's a ten-lane expressway, on a warm mid-

6

summer evening, with the sky clearing after a day of rain.

The expressway! Of course! How obvious everything is when once it's happened.

———————————————

He drives with the windows down, warm air streaming around him, swept along in a jewelled red river of tail-lights five lanes wide.

They are approaching some great metropolis. The expressway flies over quiet suburban streets with old-fashioned lamps coming on among the elms. A pagoda is silhouetted against the golden west, then a windmill with sails turning, picked out with coloured lights, then a floodlit château with pink pigs standing outside it on their hind legs, sharpening knives and holding up menus. Neon signs flash and shift, ghostly pale against the sunset, brilliant against the piled black clouds in the north. He recognizes some of them – the Pan-Am symbol, *Dagens Nyheter*, the Seven Names of God. Electric characters announce the temperature and humi-dity, closing prices on the stock market, and the latest digits reached in the computation of the value of II. There is a smell of coffee in the air. In the forecourt of a pancake house the gigantic figure of a woman revolves on top of a pylon, picked out by spotlights, standing on tiptoe, high-kicking. He cranes to catch sight of her face, and as she turns towards him he sees that it is St Julian of Norwich. 'And all shall be well,' she tells him softly, over the car radio, 'and all manner of things shall be well.'

He knows that she is right; all matter of things *will* be well in this city he is entering. He is not at all tired.

even though he has driven so far. A restless excitement stirs in him, a sense of being on the verge of deep and different things.

The expressway turns to cross water full of the redness of the sky, and there, floating on the horizon above the shining red water, are the clustered towers of the inner city, purple with distance, lights shining in a million windows – exactly as he has always known they would be. Now other freeways are converging upon his, passing above and beneath, wheeling and turning all round him. He follows the Downtown postings, up, round, through, and over; one of a thousand particles circling the orbits of a complex molecule.

When he emerges from this the towers are much closer. They rise straight up into the sky above him. He can see into some of the windows. In one room two people are dancing to music which only they can hear. In another a family is just sitting down to its evening meal. Faintly he can smell soup, and taste radishes and wine.

Now he is driving slowly along a straight street cut like a slot between the towers. It's hot. People stroll in their shirtsleeves, and sit at sidewalk cafés. One man is just taking another by the arm as he passes, and laughing in surprise. Yellow taxicabs race past, swerving in front of him, braking violently at stop lights.

He drives on until he comes to an open square with people eating at tables under the trees. High up on the other side of the square is a sign on which words pass rapidly from right to left across a bank of lights.

'Howard Baker?' say the words on the sign as Howard gets out of the car. He looks up, surprised, then glances round to see if anyone else has noticed.

'So here you are!' forms the sign smoothly. 'But don't feel any sense of anticlimax, because everyone here wants to meet you, and all sorts of parties are being arranged, and several people are going to be calling you in the morning.'

He grins, embarrassed and pleased.

'The silly buggers!' he says.

In your first few hours in a new place, while you're still dazed, before you can even really believe you've arrived, you see it more vividly and more clearly than you ever will again. Even after a few minutes – even while the porter is still showing him to his room – Howard feels that he has understood a great deal about this city. He could write a book about it.

'There's something in the air in this place!' he tells the porter. 'I really feel alive here!'

'Sure,' says the porter. 'You're really going to have yourself a good time.'

He's got brown eyes and a smiling face – the sort of man who knows his way around, and who'll fix anything for you. Howard takes to him. He feels he can talk seriously with him.

'What's happening here?' he asks him seriously. 'What's the political situation at the moment? When are the elections coming up? Are you free? What do you have to pay for a pair of men's shoes, for example? Have you been hit by inflation?'

'Don't worry,' says the porter. 'It's okay here. You don't have to worry.'

He leads Howard across little courtyards full of hibiscus, where you can hear fountains playing, and people laughing softly; along candlelit cloisters; straight across lawns with metal labels stuck in them saying 'Fellows only'.

Howard feels a great need to talk in Spanish.

9

'*Quale sono le questione politiche le piu importante in questo momento?*' he asked effortlessly. 'But this is fantastic! I've never been able to speak Spanish before, apart from a few odd phrases like *spaghetti bolognese* and *virtuosi di Roma*! And here I am just doing it, like that!'

'You can do anything here,' says the porter. 'You want to sing? Then sing! You want to dance? So dance! This is the golden land of opportunity. If I wanted to be a doctor or a lawyer, I could be one tomorrow. Just like that. Just by snapping my fingers. I could have one of the finest practices in the city. Sometimes I've thought of going into business. I could do that. No trouble. I could buy up this hotel tomorrow. I could buy up the whole block. Ride up and down in a chauffer-driven limousine, smoking big cigars. Only one thing stops me.'

'What's that?' asks Howard.

'I don't want to. I'm happy the way I am. Why fool around with money, or taking teeth out, when I might not enjoy it as much? This is what I'm used to — carrying gentlemen's bags up, turning on the lights and the air-conditioner, taking a look round to make sure everything's just so. This is the way I am, and I figure why be different? But you, you could do anything. You've got ambition, you've got drive, you're open to new experience. Have you ever thought of becoming a hotel porter, for instance?'

'No?' says Howard, astonished.

'Because remember — in this place anything's possible. Look, make a little experiment.'

He stops, and puts down Howard's bags. They are in a lobby surrounded by staircases and landings.

'Bend your knees slightly,' he tells Howard.

'What?'

'Look, like this. Now, up on tiptoe. Then — push off.'

Howard pushes off. He drifts slowly up into the air.

Sweet Dreams

Michael Frayn was born in London in 1933. He began his career as a reporter and humorous columnist, first on the *Guardian* and then on the *Observer*. He has written five novels and a number of plays, including *Alphabetical Order*, *Clouds*, *Make and Break*, *Noises Off*, and *Benefactors*. He has also translated for the theatre, mostly from the Russian, and published a philosophical work, *Constructions*. He has continued to work intermittently as a journalist, with features for the *Observer* on Cuba, Israel, Japan, and elsewhere, and with a series of personal films for BBC Television on Berlin, Vienna, Australia, Jerusalem, and the London suburbs in which he grew up.

'This is fantastic!' he says.

He drifts back towards the floor.

'I *knew* it was possible!' he calls back to the porter. 'But before I could never do it! I knew it was just a matter of getting the knack!'

'Push off from the banisters. Do frog-kicks. Force the air away underneath you with your hands.'

Howard is enchanted by the slowness with which he can move, and the smallness of the gestures which are needed to change course and height. He steers himself into the current of warm air rising above the chandelier, and is carried effortlessly upwards, past floors where people are sitting at little tables and eating ice-cream out of metal goblets. Some of them smile at him, and wave.

'This is fantastic!' he shouts back at the porter, now several floors below him. 'This is staggering! It's amazing! It's . . . well, it's fantastic!'

'Mind your head on the ceiling,' shouts the porter.

'Why don't you take off and come up here, too?'

The porter shrugs.

'Why should I?' he says. 'I'm happy where I am.'

'But it's fantastic up here!'

'It's fantastic down here.'

Howard laughs. A ridiculous thought has just occurred to him. He glides downwards, vertiginously, holding his breath at the emptiness beneath him.

'I'm sorry,' he says, as he sets foot to floor. 'That wasn't Spanish I was talking to you in. That was Italian.'

'Italian – Spanish,' shrugs the porter. 'Who cares? Here you speak any language you please, and they'll all come running.'

There's always a bad moment, Howard knows, after the porter's unlocked your room, switched everything on, drawn the curtains, and gone away with a huge tip because you had only a folder of fresh banknotes in your pocket, when you sit down helplessly and think, well, here we are, this is it, I've arrived. Now what? Shall I go down and eat in the hotel restaurant, or shall I go out? And if you're not careful you sit there blankly in the one armchair, with the curtains drawn and your bag on the stand, until it's too late to do anything.

But just before this moment arrives, as soon as the door closes on the porter, Howard notices the writing-table, and all the little giveaways which the management has arranged under the lamp – books of matches, a long-stemmed rose in water, writing-paper, and picture postcards of the hotel. The postcards absorb him at once. They show (for instance) guests dining in the hotel's famous Oak Room, with the celebrated choice of 142 dishes from all over the world, to the accompaniment of a three-piece Mariarchi band. If you tilt the card back and forth a little, the picture appears to move. The hands of the Mariarchi players strum their guitars. The forks of the diners flash from plate to mouth and back. Sommeliers reach discreetly forward to refill glasses. The waiters' spoons dig up down, up down in the great trifle on the world-famous dessert trolley. Gentlemen's jaws chomp. Ladies' smiles flash. A couple in one corner kiss discreetly over the brandy.

Howard tilts the card back and forth until he has seen the couple in the corner leave, and the manager quietly coping with a customer who refuses to pay the bill, then puts it carefully into his pocket to save for his children, who love this kind of toy. He puts four books of matches into his pocket as well. These are for his wife, who smokes. For himself he will take a handful of the pencils they always leave out for you . . . But here he makes a surprising discovery. At the top of the blotter, where the pencils should be, is a pencil-case. It's made of red plastic, and there's something familiar about it which he can't quite identify; something about the feel of its grained texture, and of the shiny red popper button on the flap . . . He pulls it open. There's something even more familiar still about the contrast between the grained texture on the outside, and the red smoothness of the inside.

Then for some reason he smells it – and at once he knows. It's his first pencil-case, that he had for his sixth birthday. For nearly thirty years it's been lost. And now it's been lovingly found again by the management of the hotel to welcome him. It has its new smell still – the perfect red plastic smell, the smell of writing numbers in arithmetic books ruled in squares; the smell it had before it got mixed up in the dust and Plasticine and tangled electric flex in the toy-drawer.

And inside the pencil-case the management has placed something even more astonishing : a propelling pencil with four different colours in it. The colours appear at little windows in the side, glimpses into the worlds of heartrending blueness and greenness, unattainable redness and blackness, that lie hidden inside the smooth nickel barrel. On the outside of the barrel, to be turned to the colour you want and slid down to push the lead into the tip, is an outer sleeve; heavy, thick, graspable, with eight shining nickel facets, alternately smooth and cross-hatched. Howard moves his fingers over the smoothness of the smooth facets, the complex texture of the hatched ones, scarcely able to absorb the pleasure that their alternation gives him. This is not a relic of his sixth birthday, or any other birthday. This is the pencil that his kindergarten teacher possessed; the pencil that made the blue ticks and the red crosses in the register; the pencil that he wept for, that his mother went all over town to find, and failed to find, because they were all gone, or not made any more, or kept for teachers, or only imagined; the pencil which he knew would make him happy, if only he possessed it, for ever more.

And here it is, its heaviness lying in his palm, his hand closing over the alternating smoothness and lininess of it.

What a hotel! He'll recommend it to everyone.

He goes to sleep with the feeling that things are going to go right for him in this town.

And enjoys a perfect night's sleep – deep, clear, and refreshing, like gliding down through sunlit water on a hot day; such a perfect night's sleep that he is entirely unconscious of how much he is enjoying it, or of its depth, clarity, and refreshingness, or its resemblance to gliding through sunlit water on a hot day; so perfect that from time to time he half wakes, just enough to become conscious of how unconscious of everything he is.

He wakes early next morning, and goes out at once, anxious to get to grips with the city. The air is still cool when he comes out on the street, and the sunlight has that soft, early-morning freshness which makes even the cars and buses seem alert and hopeful. People wearing light suits and crisp dresses are walking to work, glancing at newspapers as they go. Howard walks with them, his eyes moving from person to person, from object to object, trying to take everything in. What kind of place is this? What sort of feel does it have? Where does it remind him of? He forms a new general conclusion at every third step. Focusing on a plump man with dark hair at a bus-stop he decides the people are Latin. But – as he takes in two girls with long fair hair – there is a North European element as well. A black street-sweeper; they have a racial situation. An elegant fire-hydrant, an acceptable litter-bin, a well-thought-out pedestrian-barrier; the standards of design are high. He stops to look in a shop window. It's an electrical shop, with a shining chrome display of toasters, coffee-pots, and electric carving-knives. The prices range from 47,25 to 5.040,80. Some of the apparatus is made by Philips and Westinghouse, some by manufacturers he has never heard of. It all looks slightly unfamiliar. But good. He likes the general impression it makes.

He stops at a kiosk and buys all the better-class local papers he can find, together with an airmail edition of the *Times*, a street map, and a green Michelin guide to the city. He takes them to a café terrace in the sun, orders coffee and croissants, and starts on the papers.

He finds them very difficult to follow. The CS have walked out of the annual conference of the CDF, he reads. The CCU-CLC is split down the centre over the CGTC dispute. Theirry has declared his support for Dallapiccola but there are signs that Pugachev may be about to break off his 'Long Courtship' of Guizot. Theirry . . . Guizot . . . CDF . . . the names are all faintly familiar, and have a serious look about them. There is quite a lot about God, though, of whom even Howard has heard. '100.000 VOIENT DIEU A L'OUVER-TURE DE L'EXPO "TECHNOLOGIE PUBLICITAIRE".' 'Gott: Ohne Vertrauensvotum mach' ich nicht weiter!' 'Dieu serait contrarié par la hausse des produits laitiers.' The domestic politics in the *Times* look embarrassingly homely by comparison. 'An incomes policy' – 'the Foreign Secretary' – 'Labour back-benchers cheered' . . . how shabbily comprehensible it all seems!

He licks butter and flakes of croissant off his fingers, and turns to the Michelin, impatient to get started on actually looking at things. His eyes run quickly down the page. 'Centre administratif de l'univers . . . *Capitale des Capitales* . . . une cité fourmillante d'dées . . . ses splendours inépuisables . . . sa beauté "morale" . . . ses mille et un plasirs . . .

'UN PEU D'HISTORIE: C'est ici qu'est arrivé, vers l'an 67, selon la légende, St Jean le Théologien . . . légèrement entraîné par son enthousiasme, sans doute, il a décrit une ville "d'un or pur, semblable à du verre clair," qui était longue, large, et haute da "douze mille stades" (240km) . . . Quoi qu'il en soit, les archéologues ont découvert, sous le parking du Café Apocalypse actuel, les restes d'une porte magnifique en or et en pierres précieuses . . . (Pour la visite, s'addresser au gardien. Fermé le dimanche) . . .'

The list of things to be seen goes on for several pages, and most of them have three stars. It's suggested that you should linger on the great avenues and squares in the morning and afternoon, to see the swarms of officials and experts who administer the universe hurrying to and from their offices; or sit for a while in the shady walks of the various public gardens, and watch these same officials' wives proudly taking the baby out for an airing. There are certain bars where artists and writers are always to be seen, talking animatedly as they set the world to rights. The pageantry surrounding the court is a feast of spectacle and venerable tradition.

The museums are going to take quite a lot of time. They contain *all* the world's originals. Howard never realized – up to now he has seen only copies of the Night Watch and the Birth of Venus; indeed of everything, from electron microscopes and tinopeners to the muddle of Plasticine, string, and electric flex in the toy-drawer at home. It's a real metropolis.

He pays the check and sets out briskly, Michelin under his arm, passing newsbills for the popular papers which say:

'DIEU ET MARGARET: SE SERAIENT-ILS
BROUILLES?'

He walks along a broad, straight avenue lined with luxury shops. Chauffeurs wait at the kerb beside long, illegally-parked cars. Women with large dark glasses and small hats go by, leading dogs. Howard looks into the shop windows as he passes and sees himself walking eagerly along. He disappears briefly into revolving doors and uniformed doormen, then reappears among discreet silk ties, or cashmere sweaters and handmade brogues. He notices an odd thing about himself:

he looks *right*. He is still himself – still rather short and tubby, with a high forehead, and dry hair that turns upwards and back in the wind of his passage. He still leans forward slightly as he walks, as if he is just about to shake hands with an old friend, and he still has a slight benevolent smile about his lips. But in these surroundings the whole effect seems somehow natural. This is partly because – as he realizes with a shock – he is remarkably well dressed. His light summer suit and pale striped silk tie are for once *exactly* like the light summer suits and pale striped silk ties that everybody else is wearing. And yet, at the same time, they are entirely different. He has at last achieved his ambition to look both indistinguishable and distinctive.

Also, as he discovers after a little experiment, the windows of the shops here are constructed so that you don't have to keep looking sideways to see yourself in them. You can catch sight of yourself looking at other things than your own reflection, wearing unself-conscious expressions of interest and curiosity. He sees himself crossing the road – deftly, like a native, knowing exactly which way to look for the traffic. His shoulders are broader than he had supposed, he notices as he walks away from himself; his bottom sticks out less. He watches his expression carefully as he goes up to a beggar and puts a coin in his tin. He has always feared that he looks embarrassed or patronizing on these occasions. But not at all. He finds that he looks at the beggar intensely, as if he would like to know his life story, and smiles quite naturally.

The beggar is plainly moved, and goes on looking curiously at Howard for some moments after he has walked on.

He threads his way through narrow alleys where the sun never penetrates. Fat women and bald-headed men standing in the doorways of tiny shops make jokes to him which he can't quite understand, and shout ribaldries to each other about him – clapping him on the shoulder to indicate they're not serious, and cutting slices of cheese and sausage for him to try.

In a quiet street beside a canal small children are playing. One of them comes tottering up to him, falls, and pitches a red plastic fire-engine at his feet. Gravely he stands the child up, and restores the fire-engine. Old ladies sitting on benches under the trees beam at him.

Near the railway station he finds shops with dusty windows full of strange rubber objects; bulging, pink, obscure. Long legs and pointed breasts wait in doorways. Lips and eyelashes smile at him.

He walks along the top of ancient city walls, passing secretly among the rooftops, through a world of slates and television aerials and caged birds at dormer windows; emerges upon high places where the whole city – roofs, towers, domes, and lives – is gathered at his feet, and the immense acreage of its noise comes up to him like the murmur of the sea.

And he stops at cafés, for a sit-down with a beer or an apéritif or a coffee, without so much as noticing the prices, or whether it is too near lunchtime.

After lunch (in a little restaurant with a vine shading the tables, where the proprietor comes out for a chat, and orders him brandy on the house; 37,20, wine and service included; astonishing value) he lies down on his bed, and with delicious gradualness, watching the bars of sunlight stirring gently on the half-drawn curtains, falls asleep.

Even his dreams in this place are extraordinary.

He dreams he is sitting at the wheel of his car at the traffic-lights, unable to drive off because he can't decide whether to kiss Rose when he arrives, or whether to ask her for a cheese and chutney sandwich instead, or where to go for his holidays. His wife is standing at the window, looking out at the rain.

'But what do you feel *yourself*?' she keeps asking. 'Do you want to go back to that place in Brittany again? Or shall we borrow the Waylands' cottage? Or what?'

He can do nothing, though, because the stuffing is coming out of the armchair he is sitting in, and before anything else can happen he has to decide whether to get it re-covered or buy a new one.

'But you must have some kind of idea what sort of chair you want to spend your holidays in!' says his wife.

By this time the light is red again. So nothing can be done for another year.

In the late afternoon, as he is walking past the Little Palace (***Bramante 1512, chapel by Michelangelo, later additions by Bernini, Wren, Pugin, and van der Rohe), whistles begin to shrill, and policemen appear from nowhere to stop the traffic and hold back pedestrians from crossing the road. Howard peers over the shoulders of the people in front of him, trying to see what's going on. Beyond the palace railings in the distance a handful of white-haired old men in some kind of grotesque medieval robes emerge from an archway. Two of them are wearing spectacles, and one a hearing-aid. They form a group in the courtyard, some of them talking to each other, some walking up and down, one chatting to the policemen at the gate. Howard thinks to himself that he must write to his children tonight and tell them that he has seen his first angels. It's just the kind of thing they like to put in their newsbooks at school. He wonders if he could get postcards of them.

Suddenly a police-car emerges from the archway in the palace, its blue light flashing, followed by a closed Cadillac with tinted windows and a pennant on the wing. The two cars swing out of the palace gates, and disappear down the avenue. The angels go back inside. The policemen controlling the pedestrians beckon them across the road.

Now that Howard has thought about his children, he misses them painfully. This is the worst time of day for the solitary traveller, when the light begins to mellow, and life slows down, and the evening looms ahead. This is the moment when it comes into his mind to ask himself what he's doing in this place; to see the meaninglessness of his business there, and the hollowness of his enjoyments; to lose sight suddenly of what it is in the texture of life that has ever occupied his attention and led him forward.

But just before this happens, while the taste of melancholy on his tongue is strong enough to set off the sweetness of the place, and of his freedom to enjoy it, but not yet strong enough to overpower it, he sees the woman who is gazing at him from the balustrade of a terrace looking down on the street. For a moment they look straight into each other's eyes. Hers are dark and serious, and accept his existence. She looks away. But he doesn't hesitate. He runs straight up the stone steps leading to the terrace – it's part of a small public garden – rounds the urn at the top, and comes face to face with her, with no idea at all inside his head as to what words will emerge from his mouth.

'I beg your pardon,' he says, 'but when is lighting-up time here?'

'What?' says the woman, frowning. She has long dark hair over her shoulders, and thick dark eyebrows. She is a little alarmed.

'I feel like an ice-cream,' says Howard. He has just noticed people eating ice-cream on a café terrace across the street.

'I'm waiting for someone,' says the woman, looking round anxiously.

'Well, then, *you* could have coffee.'

'It gets dark at about eight,' she says, pulling nervously at her hair.

'You could watch out for them from across the street,' replies Howard.

'I suppose *I* could have coffee . . .' she suggests doubt-fully.

'God, I did that well!' he cries, as they sit on the café terrace sipping vermouth. 'Has anyone *ever* come up to you and introduced himself like that before?'

She shakes her head, looking at him curiously.

'No,' she says. 'Not in those words, at any rate.'

He laughs.

' "When is lighting-up time?" ' he says. 'That was an inspiration! It just came out! Honestly, I hadn't the slightest idea what I was going to say as I walked up to you. It was just seeing you like that. I knew at once that I could do it. I knew at once that I could just walk up to you and we could start talking, as if it was the most natural thing in the world. I knew you wanted me to talk to you. Perhaps you didn't know that yourself. Perhaps you *didn't* want me to talk to you. But I knew that you wanted me to talk to you *whether you wanted me to or not!* Do you see what I mean? And at once I could do it.'

She smiles slightly, and looks down at her hand as she runs a finger round the steel rim of the little marble-topped table. It is apparent to him that she has a diffi-cult nature, at once placid and turbulent, bold and re-served. He tells her this.

'Ah,' she says.

'But the effect you have on me is extraordinary! I mean, that I should be sitting here telling you that you've got a passionate nature, within ten minutes of meeting you . . .! I don't even know your name. Or perhaps I do. Let me guess. Is it . . . Rose?'

It is. Later he remembers something.

'Aren't you waiting for someone?'

'I was,' she says. He puts his hand over hers on the table.

Later still they stroll a little, among the other strolling couples in the dusk.

'Or perhaps it's this city,' he says. 'Because here I feel I can do anything at all. Do you know you can fly here? Look!'

He bends his knees, pushes off, and drifts above the heads of the passers-by.

'You just bend your knees,' he calls down to Rose. She nods, smiling.

'Come on up, then! It's fantastic!'

She pushes off and lets herself drift a few feet above the ground, holding her skirt round her knees.

'This is silly,' she says, frowning. 'Only children do this.'

'But why? It's so enjoyable!'

'Is that all you think about?' she asks disapprovingly.

They touch down, and he pushes off again, taking her arm so that she glides up with him in spite of herself. Like this they bound slowly down the boulevard, with him laughing and kicking people's hats awry as they come arcing back on to the pavement at the end of each step.

'This is a ridiculous way to behave,' she says.

'Absurd!'

'Supposing everyone went down the street like this. There'd be chaos.'

At the end of the boulevard is a square where the traffic is jammed solid. They bound out over the jam, bouncing off the roofs of cars with a hollow metallic booming noise.

'What an astonishing city this is!' he shouts to her,

24

over the noise of the hooting beneath. 'I have a feeling of sudden spiritual growth here. I feel I've developed morally to become capable of things I could never have dreamed of before. If I'd met you earlier the fact that I'm married would have made it impossible for me to take off and fly with you like this. But morally I've grown up downwards. I was 37 when I arrived. Now I'm about 32 or 31. So all this is five or six years ago. And since Felicity – that's my wife – *can't* now experience what's happening five years ago – because it's receding faster than the speed of light, and the speed of light is a constant which, as we know from Einsteinian physics, cannot be exceeded . . . Do you see what I mean?'

She smiles.

Later they have dinner together. He tells her about the pencil-case and the four-colour propelling pencil. He tells her, too, about the toy-drawer in which the pencil-case was originally lost, and the characteristic choking dusty smell it would develop as the toys in it became mixed up with each other to form a kind of solid pudding, which had to be taken out at the end of each school holidays, and separated once again into its components. He describes the toy-drawer exactly, from the rubber sealing rings out of old tobacco tins, kept to make catapults (which, with the string and the electric flex, were the principle binding agents in the mass), to the leaking paper bag of saltpetre (which may have accounted for the choking smell). The words to describe these difficult memories of confusion come to him magically – not without effort, not without searching for them, but with the assurance that each word is right, and calls forth its object exactly. She listens to him silently, sometimes looking down at his hand on the table, and lightly running her middle finger over it, from the wrist to the tip of the index finger, sometimes looking straight into his eyes. Sometimes he falls silent, too. At these moments he looks closely at each inch of her face, like a valuer frowningly examining some precious object. The skin of her face is soft and lived-in, with little wrinkles at the corners of her eyes, and beneath the lobes of her ears. She is as old as he is, and has had lovers and sadnesses, and difficulties of her own making. She tells him about her father – about how he stood on the cliffs in a flapping raincoat when she was a child and sang the whole of 'O thou that tellest Good Tidings to Zion' over the roar of the wind and surf, and about how later she could not speak to him without irritation in spite of her love for him. Exactly like himself and his own father! She tells him about the street she was brought up in, its granular asphalt pavement ridged with long wavering bulges where they had been dug up to get at the gas and water mains, and overhung by waterfalls of laburnum, with front gardens marked off by low walls, some of them in crenellated brickwork, some in pebble-dash with decorative chains dipping above them that you could set swinging, one after another, as you walked by. He knows exactly what she means – he was brought up in a street that might have been just round the corner. She tells him how she discovered Keats and Mozart and Goethe and Monet, and began to hate the laburnum and the grass verges and the swinging chains in front of the rose-beds. Just as he did. How she had a close friend at school who slept with men from the age of sixteen; how she first went to France with this friend; how she hated her first few terms at university; how she went through a wild phase of drunken parties and desperate affairs; how she plays the spinet late at night, when no one can hear, and fills the tired darkness with thin plunking antique counterpoint. He lives her life with her, year by year, seeing her become what she is. But at the same time he has an acute sense of her as being more than the object of his perception, as being another subjectivity, a self which is not his own self. He is amazed by the complex destiny which has put them before each other like this, two solid independent creatures face to face, two selves, with a common background and a common source of reference in Goethe's *Faust*.

He opens his mouth to tell her this, but she puts her finger on his lips to silence him.

'Now I must go,' she says.

And, appallingly, goes.

———————

She hurries along the street, looking straight in front of her. He has almost to run to keep up.

'You don't really have to go, do you?' he asks her anxiously. 'Who is it? Let them wait for once. Is it the person you were waiting for earlier . . . ? But we've only just met . . . ! Surely we've got time to sit down somewhere and have a coffee . . . ?'

'I'm sorry,' she says, hurrying on.

This is terrible. He is now twenty-two. He understands nothing. Women are self-contained universes, mysterious dark radio stars which work on laws entirely different from our own.

They are in a quiet part of the city, an old quarter where there are brass kicking-plates on the thresholds of the closed shops, their cross-hatchings worn almost smooth by years of polishing. In the dark shop windows snuff and hand-rolled cigarettes are discreetly displayed. They are almost the only people about. Their footsteps echo between the ancient stone buildings. From behind high walls the warm scent of flowers comes and goes; from an open window the sound of a 'cello.

'When shall I see you again?' he asks, hopelessly.

'I don't know.'

'Tomorrow?'

'Perhaps. Possibly.'

But how can this be? In this city where everything is possible, and he cuts such a figure in his light suit and striped silk tie, and is 32 and full of self-confidence, and can walk up to a girl he has never seen before and with a disarming smile ask her when lighting-up time is – how can he be wearing a maroon crew-necked sweater, and cavalry twill trousers with turnups, and be 22, and find himself running after a girl and being told that she may or may not see him tomorrow? What kind of a holiday is *that*?

They stop outside an archway closed by a heavy wooden gate. Rose pulls at a handle, and somewhere a bell dances.

'What time tomorrow, then?' he asks. 'Shall we meet at the same place? Or shall I come here?'

'Tomorrow's a bit awkward,' she says, twisting her shoe back and forth on the ground. 'Perhaps one day next week?'

Next week . . . ? He gazes at her, hating the way she twists her foot, hating the way she brushes awkwardly at her hair, hating the way her jaw is just too square and her eyebrows are just too thick.

'But I love you,' he says, in a low, unsuccessful voice, 'What did you say?'

'I said, how about the day after tomorrow, then?'

Slow footsteps approach on the other side of the door. A bolt rattles. She comes quickly up to him and smiles into his face.

'Tomorrow, then,' she says. 'Perhaps.'

She takes his face between her hands and kisses him on the lips. A picket opens in the gate, and an old man waits impassively while she runs inside, into the light. The picket shuts.

Now he understands what he is doing aged 22. He walks back across the town, drifting off the ground at every other step, floating the length of whole streets. He looks down into the gardens hidden everywhere behind the patched and crumbling walls. A warm night breeze rustles in the dark trees, and bears him along. Somewhere a different bell begins to sound midnight, and from all over town, far and near, other bells join in.

He is transfigured. Every cell in his body is charged and polarized. Like a laser beam, he could pass through solid objects. And indeed, watched curiously by a solitary policeman below, he passes right through a library (**) by Hawksmoor, and emerges on the other side coughing slightly from the dust in the books.

'There's a gentleman waiting to see you,' says the porter, when he gets back to the hotel. He indicates a figure sitting in a corner of the darkened, empty lobby. Howard goes across to the man curiously, since he doesn't know anyone in this city. But long before he reaches him he recognizes him – from the way he's sitting, sprawled back in an armchair with his feet on a coffee-table, reading an ancient *Amazing Science Fiction*; from his spectacles and rumpled hair; from the fact that he's taken his shoes and socks off to cool his feet, and tossed them down on the coffee-table; from the way he doesn't look up, even as Howard comes right up to him, goggling head leading the way, unable to believe his eyes.

'Phil!' he cries. 'Phil Schaffer!'

'Hi,' says Phil, without interest, looking up briefly

from his magazine.

'What are *you* doing here?'

'Putting a curse on your old toenail clippings,' says Phil, licking his finger and turning the page. 'Didn't you get my message?'

'No? What message?'

'I left a note on the electric sign opposite.'

'Oh. That was you?'

'Of course it was me. Who else do you know who'd leave a note on an electric newscaster?'

Howard sits down, staring at him, unable to take it in. Whenever Phil's there Howard can't take things in.

'You didn't say anything about coming here,' he says. 'I mean, it's thousands of miles . . .'

'How did you think you were going to get by without me to explain everything to you?' asks Phil reasonably. 'Have you got any idea how this city works? What have you been doing all day – walking round with the Michelin, looking at churches?'

Howard laughs. He looks at Phil affectionately, unable to think of anything to say. Phil continues to read *Amazing Science Fiction*.

'The only times you ever make any effort to think,' says Phil, 'are when you're trying to understand what I'm saying. You don't want to give up thinking, do you? It's your thinking that got you into this place!'

'Yes, well . . .' says Howard slowly. He always speaks slowly to Phil.

'You've got to have someone to make a fool of you. You'd be unbearable otherwise. You wouldn't be able to stand the sight or sound of yourself after a week.'

'No, well . . .'

'Anyway, I've obviously got to be here if you're going to be leading the good life, since I'm a major component of it.'

Howard rubs his forehead.

'But what I don't understand,' he says, 'is exactly

how it all . . . fits together. Do we both just happen to *share* the same good life?'

Phil lowers *Amazing Science Fiction*.

'Christ!' he cries. 'This isn't *my* idea of the good life! What? Some bloody great luxury hotel, with waiters in dickeys, and bellhops covered in buttons?'

'Oh, come on, Phil! Be fair! It's not that sort of hotel at all. It's rather, well, a rather jocky old family establishment, with, I don't know, lots of different levels everywhere, and ancient baths . . . Honestly, they're very friendly here. They really seem to *enjoy* running a hotel – I had a long talk with the porter . . . And the food is first-class.'

'Howard,' says Phil sadly, 'you are the collective imagination of the middle classes compressed into one pair of trousers.'

He gazes at the ceiling for some time.

'If this were *my* life,' he says softly, 'I'd be living in a hotel made of chocolate sponge cake and organ music. I'd be eating fried X-rays for breakfast.'

'I haven't done so badly,' says Howard. 'I've learnt to fly. Look.'

He pushes himself out of his armchair, and shoots rather awkwardly upwards, catching his foot against an overhead light. Phil watches him expressionlessly.

'I can get older and younger, too,' calls Howard down to him. 'At the moment I'm 37, right? Now, watch.'

But with Phil looking at him he somehow can't get below 35. Phil picks up his magazine again.

'Jesus wept,' he says. 'If it had been me I'd have learnt to be transmitted as microwaves by now, and bounced off Jupiter. I'd have given birth to twins and discovered what song the Sirens sang, and vaporized and condensed and fallen as snow all over central Calcutta.'

Howard sinks back into his chair. The world feels very stable and familiar, with Phil there to insult him. They will go about the city in the weeks to come, and

Phil will point out things behind doorways and up courtyards that he'd never noticed, and explain how the whole set-up of the city is really a conspiracy, and read out public notices in a voice that makes them suddenly ridiculous, and persuade him to believe preposterous stories.

'I can see what your idea is,' says Phil, with sudden gloom. 'I'm to be slightly too clever, the hare to your tortoise, so that you can plod past me halfway round the course and make me look a fool.'

Howard laughs guiltily. The idea was just about to occur to him.

The last glowing embers in the fireplace knock as they settle among the ash. Somewhere a clock has struck two, or three. Howard and Phil are both half-asleep.

'I didn't really expect it to be like this,' says Howard. 'I mean, I didn't really expect *anything*. I never thought about it. But if I *had* expected anything, I should have expected something a little more . . . I don't know . . . abstract. I thought that what went on here was more sort of . . . contemplation. More sort of . . . oneness with the infinite, sort of thing.'

'Howard,' says Phil, 'how long do you think you could have sat here being at one with the infinite before you'd felt your bottom aching and your scalp itching?'

Howard imagines himself at one with the infinite.

'I didn't think I'd have a bottom or a scalp,' he says.

'No bottom? What would you have sat on? No scalp? What would have kept your brains from falling out?'

'Well . . .'

'Don't tell me you didn't think you were going to

have any brains!'

'Well . . .'

'Howard, without brains you'd have gone out of your *mind*! After all, what do you actually *like*? What do you actually *enjoy*? Not contemplation, Howard. Not being in touch with the infinite. What you like is prawn biriani and apple crumble; getting up late on Sunday and reading the papers in your dressing-gown; looking at your insurance policies; being taken for an academic; picking food out from between your teeth with a sharpened matchstick.'

'I thought I'd be different here.'

'Would you *like* to be different?'

Howard thinks, picking food out from between his teeth with a sharpened matchstick.

'No,' he says finally.

'Well, then.'

They're all here, it turns out, all his friends. The Chases, the Waylands, the Chyldes, the Esplins – they've all found old houses in the south-western and nothern suburbs of the city, and done them up, and rung to invite Howard to dinner. Luci Hayter is here, whose husband went off with the girl in market research. So is Charles Aught, that rather camp man in advertising, who writes poems and art-criticism, and whose correspondence with his fellow-critic Elwyn West was auctioned at Sotheby's and fetched £25. Bill Goody has arrived (the Labour MP, who will almost certainly get a junior ministry next time round). Even Francis Fairlie, the man they all joke about because he can never make up his mind to marry or to start a serious career or to buy a house or to do anything else that may define and announce his character to the world – even Francis Fairlie has managed to get himself here!

'We couldn't leave you here on your own,' says Prue Chase, as Howard kisses her and hands a bottle of wine to Roy, her husband. 'We knew you'd get all lonely and homesick.'

'Oh God!' says Howard. 'You didn't all move here just because of *me*?'

'When we heard you were here we thought what fun it would be,' says Roy urbanely. 'We're very grateful to you.'

'*Dear* Howard!' says Prue. 'It *is* lovely to see you!'

She is a small, pious, affectionate girl of sharp intelligence, all of it devoted to the cherishing and advancement of her friends. Howard hugs her, and has to look away for a moment, he is so moved.

'Come and have a quick tour of the house,' she says, taking his arm, 'before we go in and meet the others.'

The house moves him, too, its style is so familiar in spite of its strangeness. When the Chases found it, it was a home for unmarried mothers. Now the walls are white and the floors sealed. Carpets and cushions glow in warm colours against the white paintwork and the pale yellow wood, and little pools of lamplight draw the eye to books and magazines, and flowers, and elegant chromium toys illustrating the Law of the Diffusion of Gases and the Uncertainty Principle.

'You can just see the sea from the nursery,' explains Prue, 'and if you stand on the loo and look out of that little window you can see all those cloverleaf intersections you drove over on the way in. You're not going to believe this, but we got this place for 399.000.000,00!'

When she takes him into the living-room there is a kind of roar, and a man emerges from the background of people and easy chairs, and advances upon Howard, his arms outstretched, his deep, dark eyes raking back

34

and forth over Howard's face, soaking it in with eager amazement. This is Michael Wayland, who appears on television a lot, and who as a consequence can never remember anything unless it's written on the Autocue, or held up beside the lens in front of him. He won't remember Howard's name, for instance.

'Howard!' he cries. He has! But this is the most flattering thing that has ever happened to Howard!

'Well done,' murmurs Prue.

Michael holds Howard by the upper arms, to take in his corporeal presence through his finger-tips, and to keep him at the right distance for gazing at in astonishment.

'But, Howard, this is extraordinary!' he says. 'That you should be over here too!'

A shout of laughter goes up from the room. Michael looks round at them all.

'Oh God,' he says. 'Have I done it again?'

'I don't *believe* it!' gasps Prue. 'Michael, the reason we all *moved* here was that Howard was here already!'

'Oh Christ,' says Michael, smiling, pleased with himself.

'You don't realize,' says Myra, Michael's wife, from the far end of the sofa, 'the fantastic thing is that we went through all this scene twenty minutes ago, in the car on the way here. "Don't forget," I said, "that *Howard Baker's* going to be there." "Howard Baker's over here?" he shouted. He almost ran us into the back of a streetcar.'

Michael laughs. Howard laughs. Prue and Roy laugh. They are all happy that nothing has changed. Even the other two guests laugh – a woman called Pattie whose husband has just left her, and a man whose name Howard doesn't quite catch. 'He lives just down the road,' explains Prue. 'We thought you'd like to meet one of the natives, in case you haven't already. As a matter of fact he was at Cambridge just after us.'

Howard is deeply moved. There is always a woman at the Chases' dinner parties whose husband has just left her. There is always a man from just down the road, or the basement flat, or the office, whose name Howard doesn't quite catch, and who was up at Cambridge just after all the rest of them.

The meal starts with *taramasalata*.

'I'm sorry,' says Prue. 'I *always* serve *taramasalata*.'

'Yes,' says Howard, contentedly.

The next course is *gigot aux haricots*.

'I think you've had this at our house, too, haven't you?' says Prue.

'Yes,' sighs Howard. 'Many, many times.'

They eat. They drink. They talk. Howard can hear his own voice, talking smilingly, deeply, effortlessly, about secondary education and the nature of human happiness and the price of houses. A sense of well-being, of transformation and enlightenment, penetrates to the very marrow of his bones. He has a mystical experience. Each of his friends around the table, he realizes, is surrounded with a kind of aura. Their faces emanate a radiance, though whether he actually sees this with his eyes or knows it by some sort of deductive process he is not entirely sure. The radiance is the manifestation of their virtues; of their industriousness, their honesty, their interest in the appearance of the world, their pleasure in life, their unchangingness, their being who they are.

Even the man whose name Howard didn't catch, and who was at Cambridge just after him, is glowing faintly.

Prue is almost incandescent.

When people speak, their words emerge in illuminated manuscript, glowing with gold and angelic blue, tangled with flowers and tiny peasants labouring in the yellow corn.

'You must have been up with the famous Ord Gaunt?'

36

says the man whose name Howard didn't quite catch, and the dense Middle English blackletter in which the words are uttered exactly matches their resonant profundity.

'Yes, we were,' says Prue, 'and he wore luminous green socks even then.'

The words 'luminous green socks' are luminous, green, socklike.

They all laugh at the sight. Each laugh, observes Howard, looking chiefly at the laughter emerging from himself, is round and polished, as if cast in weathered bronze. Their shoulders shake, hinging up and down on well-oiled ball-and-socket joints made of stainless steel.

They have apple crumble, of course. Then Howard sits back and tells them about the terrible balls-up he made of his arrival in the city. He is famous for the balls-ups that seem to happen around him, and for the modest, humorous accounts he gives of them. They all listen with smiles beaten out of soft gold already on their lips.

———

As soon as he looked out of the window on the morning after he arrived (he tells them) and saw what the place was like, he realized that it was based on the tutorial system. Somewhere there would be a tutor waiting to see him – some easy-going, amiable man, not old, but a few years older than himself, with whom he could drink sherry on slightly deferential terms, and to whom he could apply for permission to hold parties, keep a car, and ride to hounds. Clearly his first task was to call on him and announce his arrival.

It wasn't easy to find out who his tutor was supposed to be. He walked all over the city, looking for wind-swept gateways and corridors with notice-boards in them. Every time he found one he held all the flapping notices down one by one, and read through lists of hockey teams, and announcements of meetings to be held by religious societies. At last he found a neatly-typed sheet of crested notepaper which said: 'Mr Brice will see freshmen in C4 between 11.00 a.m. and 1.00 p.m.'

Mr Brice, it turned out when he got to C4, was not older than himself at all. In fact he was about ten years younger – a chubby young man with a very smoothly-shaven pink face, bulging urbanely under the jaw. He was married, with two children, Howard discovered later, but was on bad terms with his wife, a French girl whom he had met when she was at one of the English language schools in the city. He often put his pupils off from tutorials because he was at the television studios, smilingly outlining rather shocking views about constitutional history, and the role of the trade unions. All this was by the way, however, except that it lent background and depth to the smile he gave Howard as he shook hands.

'My name's Bill,' he said. 'I'm the chap you come and see if you get pregnant, or whatever. Now, to more serious business.'

And with that he turned towards the window and sank to his knees.

Now, this was Howard's first day in the place (he reminded the Chases and their guests, preparing them dramatically for what was to come), and he had some vague impression at the back of his mind, left over per-haps from books he had read and films he had seen, that it was at bottom some kind of *ecclesiastical* institu-tion. So as soon as he saw Bill Brice sink chubbily to his knees, he jumped to the conclusion that some brief word of informal prayer was going to be said.

Had this been any other occasion, he would have lowered his head respectfully and more or less closed his eyes, watching Bill Brice out of the corner of them so as to know when to open them again, and murmuring amen where appropriate. He had a genuine respect for religious feeling. He had even experienced it himself once or twice, particularly while doing the outline plans for a church he had designed as part of a new mixed-density, mixed-income neighbourhood scheme, which had been well reviewed in the journals.

But since it was his first day in the place, he was particularly anxious to make a good impression, and to demonstrate his eagerness to accept the spirit of the institution. Also there was something decidedly impressive about the sight of Bill Brice kneeling there — so young, so overweight, so ambitious, on such premature bad terms with his wife, and yet so humble and submissive, with the toecaps of his suède desert boots turned over, and a drawing-pin sticking disarmingly in the heel of one of them.

So he got down on his knees, too, and rested his elbows on Bill Brice's coffee-table, and closed his eyes completely.

This was the sight that Bill Brice saw when he smilingly turned round, holding the fresh bottle of sherry which he had been kneeling to get out from under the window-seat.

Oh God, thought Bill Brice (said Howard), a religious nut! And smilingly he remained kneeling, as a mark of genuine respect for Howard's beliefs. Genuine respect, in his experience, was the only way of dealing with one's students' more repellent religious and political enthusiasms.

His intention was to remain on his knees for about

ten or fifteen seconds, and then to rise, saying smilingly, 'Well, then . . .' or words to that effect. But the appearance of Howard when he came into the room must have impressed him in spite of himself – the bulging clear blue eyes, the eager lean of the body forward, the anxiety on the face to understand the world around him. Because when, after seven or eight long seconds of genuine respect, he saw Howard looking at him out of the corner of his eye, he hastily hid the bottle of sherry behind his back and bowed his head.

They remained like this for a long time.

They were still like it when Sid Cornish, the Professor of Artificial Intelligence, put his head round the door to ask Bill Brice who he should see about getting on television.

'I do beg your pardon,' he said, and withdrew.

The interruption gave the two kneeling men a chance to look up, and to see each other looking up. They got to their feet, drank their sherry, smiling a lot, and never went near each other again.

But Sid Cornish, who was a serious atheist, could not get the sight of the two kneeling men out of his mind. What? Bill Brice? The television iconoclast? The smiler with the sherry bottle? Now glimpsed at prayer with a pupil? He told everyone he met, pulling a maliciously funny face to represent Bill Brice's holy expression. A week later he was in the chair at a meeting of the Humanist Society when he suddenly had a vision of Bill looking down at him from the moulding in the corner of the ceiling with a crown of thorns on his head, and a look of sweet forgiveness on his face; whereupon he stood up and made a long, confused speech about the hunger for God that gnawed inside each of us, however stiff-necked and jeering we might be; which caused great embarrassment to all those present, and even greater embarrassment later to progressive theologians on the staff, who felt that such old-fashioned emotive conversions could only undo all their good work.

But eventually it led to several notable improvements in the arrangements for the early detection of mental ill-health among faculty members.

Everyone round the table listens intently to the story — the Chases, the Waylands, the Chyldes, the Kessels, the Bernsteins, Charles Aught, Luci Hayter, Rayner Keat, and Francis Fairlie who is still hesitating about what life to commit herself to — a great audience stretching back into the dim recesses of the room, a densely-cultivated field growing faces. They are absolutely silent in the dramatic passages. They roar with laughter at the funny bits. They love the way the story trails away into the postcript about improvements to the mental health service.

'That's a real Howard Baker story!' they cry, when he has finished. 'It would happen to Howard! Only Howard could turn a glass of sherry into a religious revival!'

Howard looks down at his plate, grinning, and pressing a few crumbs of cheese on to his fingers to nibble. He is emanating quite a powerful golden light himself, he notices.

'There's a certain special sort of Howard Baker modesty,' says Roy Chase.

'A kind of innocence,' says Charles Aught.

'You just have to look at him,' says Luci Hayter, 'and you know he's going to leap with modest eagerness to the wrong conclusion.'

'As a matter of fact,' says Howard suddenly, 'when you think about it, I can't really have known what was going on in Bill Brice's mind – or in Professor Cornish's. I think, to be absolutely honest, I must have made all those bits up. And I believe the meeting of the Humanist Society which Cornish is chairing isn't until next Tuesday.'

Everyone rocks with laughter at this admission. He can see them, all down the table, leaning forwards over their plates, then back in their chairs, an irregular series of nodding heads like a shop window full of sipping chicken toys. He grins at the effect he has produced, and picks up more cheese crumbs on his finger.

'Isn't that just like Howard?' says Barratt Kessel, 'to blurt out that sort of confession? If any of the rest of us realized we'd improved a story we'd been telling, we'd just keep quiet about it.'

With a shock Howard now suddenly sees another shortcoming in his story. They don't have tutors in this place; it's not that kind of place at all. He must have made the whole thing up from start to finish. He now recalls seeing a painter on his knees in a shop doorway and thinking, wouldn't it be funny if I, as a newcomer to this city, misunderstood the situation, and, anxious to please, knelt beside him . . . ? What he has done is to supply himself with a ridiculous experience by the telling of which he could entertain several hundred people, *without* having to undergo the dispiriting strain of suffering it first. For a moment he feels worried about the ethics of this. But then he asks himself if people would have enjoyed the story any more had it been true, and if they would have achieved any greater insight into themselves and their destinies. Of course not. In any case, they don't know it wasn't true. Howard realizes that he has hit upon a radical solution to one of the main problems in enjoying a satisfactory life-style. He has discovered how to enjoy his life without being seen to.

He stands up and taps on the table for silence, intending to announce this new discovery, in the hope that it will cause yet more laughter, and increase his reputation for honesty still further.

Everyone round the table falls silent and looks at him, poised to laugh again.

'Why don't we have coffee next door?' he says, and leads the way, amidst laughter and applause.

For he has realized something else, in the moment of inspiration between standing up and beginning to speak: that the aesthetic effect of honesty depends upon restraint in its application.

'Barratt was just telling us the other night at the Goodys',' says Prue, as she pours coffee in the living-room, 'about how he had lunch with God the other day.'

'Oh, really?' says Howard, intrigued.

'Do tell Howard about it,' Prue urges.

'There's honestly nothing to tell,' says Barratt Kessel, embarrassed. 'You make it sound as if there was just me. There were ten of us, altogether. I was sitting be-tween the principal of a college for police women and a rather saucy lady novelist.'

'This was at the Palace?'

'Yes. It was just one of these regular lunch-parties he has so that he can keep in touch with people he wouldn't otherwise meet. It wasn't anything special.'

'I thought he didn't in fact live in the Palace?' objects Francis Fairlie. 'Someone in television told me he lived in an ordinary flat by the Park, with nothing but a secret service man lurking in the lobby.'

'Oh, nonsense, Francis,' says Charles Aught. 'He lives on the sixteenth floor of the RCA building. He's

43

got the whole floor. He gives terrible parties up there — I know a girl who's been to them. All white sofas and Kokoschkas and rather smart young men who write rock shows.'

'Well, I don't know,' says Barratt. 'This lunch thing was at the Palace.'

They all wait for him to go on, while appearing as if they do not care whether he goes on or not.

'Well, go on,' says Howard. 'What was he like?'

Barratt sighs.

'I know you're all going to take the piss out of me if I tell you what I honestly thought.'

'Don't be silly,' says everyone.

'Well,' says Barratt heavily, 'I thought he was very nice.'

Everyone at once begins to take the piss out of him.

'Well, I'm sorry,' says Barratt irritably, 'but he was.'

'Of course he was,' says Charles Aught soothingly. 'That's his job. But what *else* was he? This girl I know thinks he's rather camp.'

Barratt makes a helpless gesture, as if trying to catch a word out of the air.

'I don't know,' he says. 'He was very relaxed and friendly. He told some quite funny stories. He was . . . well, he was nice.'

They all burst out laughing.

'For a start he got my name right.'

Applause.

'Well, plenty of people *don't*,' says Barratt. 'Also he knew all about the work I was doing. And all about my row with Fred Hattersley.'

'And whose side was he on?' asks Bill Goody. 'Yours or Fred's?'

'Oh, for heaven's sake! He wasn't on anyone's *side*. He just looked at me and said something like, "How's my friend Mr Hattersley, then?" sort of thing. And he had a kind of little smile on his face as he said it.'

They all have little smiles on their faces.

'Barratt,' says Bill Goody, 'you're a pushover. Here you are, the great founder of housing trusts, the great battler for the homeless, the great righter of wrongs, the only humanist saint we know. We send you in to do battle with the enemy, and what happens? You come out with a moist look in your eyes, saying, "He knew my name!"'

Barratt jiggles his foot, looking anywhere but at Bill.

'It hasn't changed my opinions,' he says. 'I'm still a humanist.'

'At this rate,' grins Bill, 'we're still going to have a theocracy here a hundred years from now.'

'Well,' says Barratt stiffly, 'I can't help admiring someone who really does his homework. If we all did our jobs as well as that perhaps it wouldn't *matter* about it being a theocracy.'

They all look down into their brandy, embarrassed at the turn the conversation has taken.

'This girl I know,' says Charles Aught, trying to be cheerful, 'thinks it's really a woman dressed up.'

'You should have been here,' Howard tells his wife next morning, as they sit over their second cup of coffee on one of the upper terraces. Their house, Carceri, is a complex world of ancient stone galleries and courtyards, with weird (and scheduled) spiral staircases that you go up only to find yourself on the floor below the one you started on – an old dungeon perched among the treetops on a hillside overlooking the city, which they found by a miracle, and had converted. The sun is shining. Felicity is lying back with her eyes closed, and her face lifted to the light. Her long legs and bare feet are brown; her eyebrows and the down on her arms shine pale gold. Pigeons are purling in the trees. Beyond the branches, the traffic of the city flows endlessly; complex, remote, silent. The children are at school. The school is many-windowed, relaxed, colourful, with a good social mix and high academic standards. It's reached by a pedestrian walkway through the treetops, well away from all roads. They got their children into it by a miracle.

'Barratt was there,' says Howard, 'making sure everyone knew he'd just had lunch with God.'

Felicity's lips bend into a smile.

'Everyone was sending him up,' says Howard. 'It was terrible. You really should have been there. The *Waylands* were there – of course. Bill Goody asked Michael if he'd ever met God himself. " I *think* so," said Michael. "I think the name rings a bell." '

Felicity laughs quietly, without opening her eyes. Then she compresses her lips doubtfully.

'All right,' says Howard, smiling to himself, on the side of his face away from her, in case she opens her eyes, 'I made that bit up. But he did ask after you. "Where's the lovely Lady Catherine?" he said when I arrived. The last thing he said when I left was, "Tell Jean I'm still as much in love with her as ever." '

She puts her hand over his. He looks at her.

'There was no one there as beautiful as you,' he says. 'Luci Hayter looked as if she'd been up every night for a week. And I don't know what Prue was wearing. I think she'd knitted it herself out of old pieces of string she'd saved from the children's birthday presents.'

The sun grows hotter moment by moment. An aircraft passes high overhead.

'Francis Fairlie was there. He said he'd been meaning to invite us to dinner ever since he arrived. I think the only thing that's holding him up is making up his mind

46

whether to get married first, and have a wife sitting down the other end of the table.'

Felicity turns on to her stomach. She has no clothes on, Howard notices. Her buttocks look like two golden apples in the sun, wrinkled, like ripe apples, where they meet the top of her legs.

'I like our friends,' says Howard. 'We get a lot of pleasure out of them. But then I suppose they do out of us. Somewhere out there Michael Wayland is saying to his wife, "God, when what's-that-man's-name began telling that enormously long story about how he made a fool of himself crawling round the floor on his hands and knees, which he obviously found so funny, I thought I'd *die*." It's good to feel that one gives pleasure.'

Bees hum. From somewhere far away comes the drone of a mower, and the smell of the cut grass.

'*Did* you tell a story about crawling around on your hands and knees?' asks Felicity.

'I'm afraid I did.'

'I don't know that one.'

'No. I was making it up as I went along. I got it all back to front, and couldn't think of a punchline. It didn't seem to matter, though. *They* all thought it was marvellous. Thought it was the funniest thing since the invention of piles.'

On an impulse he leans across and takes a bite out of her righthand buttock. It is as he had imagined – crisp, sweet, and juicy. Her lips curl back from her teeth with pleasure. She takes his hand, and gently crushes each of his fingers in turn between her lips, like buttered asparagus.

Matthew, the six-year-old, leans against Howard's chair, scuffing his feet about and reading from his Janet and John book, *On We Plod*.

'Janet and John go for a walk,' he reads. 'They go for a walk with their Father. Who is this they see? It is Tim and Topsy. Tim and Topsy are going for a walk, too. They are going for a walk with their Father.'

'Good,' says Howard, thinking about teatime.

' "Hello, Tim and Topsy," say Janet and John.

' "Hello, Janet and John," say Tim and Topsy.

' " Hello, Mr . . . Aeroplane . . ." '

Howard squints over his son's shoulder.

' "Hello, Mr Wayland," ' he prompts. 'Mr Wayland! That's funny. We know someone called Mr Wayland, don't we?'

' "Hello, Mr Wayland," says Father,' reads Matthew.

' "Hello, Mr Um," says Mr Wayland.'

Howard looks over Matthew's shoulder again. He bursts out laughing.

'What?' demands Matthew suspiciously.

'Nothing. That's right! Mr Um. It's very funny, that's all. Felicity, can you hear this? Go on, Matt.'

'See,' reads Matthew, 'Mr Wayland has forgotten their names. Mr Wayland is not good at remembering things. Father is good at remembering things. Janet and John are good at remembering things. Even Tim and Topsy are good at remembering things.

'See, Mr Wayland has a funny look on his face. He thinks a friend will come along. He thinks his friend will not know Father. He thinks he will have to say, "Do you know Mr Um?" '

Howard laughs.

'Are you listening to this, Felicity?' he asks.

'He thinks that Father will be sad,' reads Matthew. 'He thinks that Janet and John will be sad.

'But Janet and John do not care whether Mr Wayland knows their name. They do not care 4p. Father does not care. He does not care 5p.

'Here are Pat and Pete. They are out for a walk with their Father.

'See, now Mr Wayland is running away.

' "Goodbye, Mr Wayland. Goodbye, Tim. Goodbye, Topsy." '

Matthew puts his marker in and closes the book. Howard runs his hand through the boy's hair.

'Very well read, Matt,' he says. 'Isn't he getting on well, Flic?'

Matthew makes his clumsy face, and moves his feet about.

'That's what I think is so good about this school,' says Howard to Felicity. 'They give them stuff to read which has really got some relevance to the children's life. Michael Wayland is an actual figure in their mythology.'

'They didn't give them that,' says Felicity. She is intent upon the picture she is painting, a luminous, finely-detailed portrait of a myoglobin molecule. 'Matt wrote it.'

'What?' says Howard, not understanding.

'Me and another boy,' says Matthew. 'It was our project. But Miss Sinclair had to help us, because we couldn't spell "Mr Wayland".'

'How do you mean, you wrote this?' demands Howard, taking the book and turning it over in his hands. 'It's printed! It's published by Ginn and Co., Educational Publishers!'

'Yes, well,' says Matthew, 'me and Kevin Williams writ it – that was *our* project. Then two of the girls.

Alexandra Saunders and Karen Holt, their project was to be literary agents and find a publisher for it.'

Howard gazes at Matthew tenderly. He has under-estimated him.

'What?' demands Matthew, frowning, and turning his feet over sideways.

Downstairs the ten-year-old and the eight-year-old are quietly occupied in running three of the old dungeons together to make a games room. Upstairs in the nursery the baby is tearing up *The Anatomy of Melancholy*, and eating it page by page.

They're good kids.

For dinner they have *taramasalata*, *gigot aux haricots*, and apple crumble. They eat outside on the terrace, it's so warm, by candlelight, with the lights of the city spread out in front of them – a sea of lights, twinkling in the uneven layers of warm air like a still sea shimmering and glittering. Currents move in the sea – the lights of traffic streams flowing and eddying. Somewhere beyond the city brush-fires are burning, hazing the horizon, and lighting the haze with a faint uneven reddish glow.

'They've got three thousand firemen up there in the hills,' says Felicity, watching it all dreamily. 'There was something about it on the news. A lot of people have lost their homes.'

The moon comes up through the smoke, pale copper, veined, enormous.

It's very peaceful.

Just as Howard is scraping the last spoonful of apple crumble out of the bowl, a thought strikes him. He gazes at Felicity in astonishment, his mouth open, the scraping spoon in his hand stilled.

'What's the matter?' asks Felicity, alarmed.

'I've just remembered something . . .'

But how can he ever have forgotten it? Was it the Chases' dinner party that put it out of his mind? Or the sunlight on the terrace all day? Or the warm golden fatness of the drenched haricot beans, and the pale smoky moon?

'I'm in love!' he explains.

Felicity gazes at him, her eyes wide open.

'I can't eat,' says Howard. 'I just have this terrible fluttering in my stomach the whole time. I can't sleep. I don't know what's happening to me – I feel as if I'm walking round in a dream. If I'm not careful I'm going to step in front of a car, or something.'

Felicity goes on staring at him in astonishment. Then she takes his hand.

'Poor love!' she says. 'Why didn't you tell me before?'

'I forgot.'

'You must be exhausted. Go and lie down. I'll bring you an aspirin and whisky.'

'I *can't* lie down!' cries Howard. 'I can't even *sit* down!'

He jumps up and begins to walk up and down the terrace. Felicity watches him with her eyebrows raised in an expression of tender, slightly comical concern.

'I'm sorry,' he says, running his hand desperately through his hair. 'I didn't mean to shout. It's not your fault. I don't know where I am with this girl, that's the trouble. One moment she's kissing me, and the next she's telling me she can't see me till next week. One day I'm walking with her beside the river, and I've got my arm round her shoulders, and she's put her arm round my waist, and we laugh at everything, and stop every few yards to kiss, and think, this is *fantastic*! It can't go on like this! And it doesn't, because she suddenly rushes off, and I have to run after her, shouting about when am I going to see her again, and jumping out of people's way into the gutter.'

Felicity laughs.

'You'll just have to be firm with her,' she says. 'Sweep her off her feet.'

'I *keep* sweeping her off her feet,' he complains. 'But then she keeps getting back on them again.'

'You always dealt with me quite effectively.'

'But I knew where I was with you!' he says irritably. 'You're a completely different sort of person!'

She sits in silence, smiling to herself. He leans over the rail of the terrace, moodily banging his knuckles against the bricks.

'Sorry,' he says finally. 'But you must see I'm a bit on edge. It's no good making fatuous suggestions . . . It would be better if you concentrated on sewing some buttons on my shirts. Half my shirts have got buttons missing now! How can I go out and pursue a love-affair wearing a shirt with no buttons on it! What on earth is she going to think? No wonder I'm not getting anywhere when I have to spend half my time holding my tie in place to cover the gap! I get no support, that's the trouble. I have to do every damned thing for myself. Other men's wives try to *help* them a little. They take pride in their husband's success . . .'

She comes over and puts her arm round his shoulders protectively.

'I wish you wouldn't do that,' he says. 'I'm obviously trying to have a row with you. Oh God – can't I even have a row with you now? What am I supposed to do – have rows with my friends? Or bottle all my aggression up and let it turn into high blood pressure? Aren't I to have *any* pleasure in life *at all*?'

She strokes his hair.

'I know what you're thinking,' he says. 'You're thinking this is all rather comical, aren't you?'

'A bit,' she says gently.

'Funny that I can always tell what you're thinking, isn't it? I can read you like a book – some book I've read six times already. That's one of the things I like about *her*. I never have the slightest idea what she's thinking. I never know what she's going to do next. It's such a relief! It gives me some slight interest in life.'

She kisses his ear. He sighs.

'Why are you behaving so aggressively?' he demands. 'Why are you making a scene like this? You're not . . . you're not *jealous*, are you? You must realize that I've got it all worked out in my head so that this doesn't have any bearing on you at all.'

'I assumed you'd got it worked out somehow,' she murmurs.

'Of course I have. I've got a clear understanding in- side my head that this business is taking place before I ever met you.'

She picks up his hand and kisses the knuckles.

'Don't worry,' she says. 'I'm not jealous.'

'Yes, you are,' he replies. 'I know when you're jealous. Don't deceive yourself. God, no wonder I'm driven to go out and have affairs! Jealous scenes every time I come home . . .'

She rubs his knuckles silently, gazing at the lights below them.

'You *are* jealous,' he says, looking at her closely. 'Aren't you? Or *aren't* you? You *aren't*, are you? You don't care a damn! It doesn't matter tuppence to you whether I go off and have affairs with other people or not . . . !'

Later, in bed, she puts her head on his shoulder and in a very small voice apologizes. The whole scene was her fault, she sees that now. He puts his arms round her, and insists that he was partly to blame as well. His generosity moves them both. Meltingly they eat at each other, like two carnivorous ice-creams.

So when he sees Rose staring at him with her dark serious eyes among the crowds on the staircases in the interval (this is at a concert) he doesn't hesitate for a moment, but goes straight up to her.

'Excuse me,' he says, 'but do you know if they're going to play the violin concerto with the original cadenzas?'

'What?' says Rose, frowning.

'Would you like some coffee?' asks Howard. He has just noticed they are serving coffee on the next floor up.

'I'm looking for someone,' says Rose.

'I feel like a coffee myself.'

'Don't they always play Mozart's cadenzas?'

'You could look for them while you're drinking the coffee.'

She looks round desperately, tugging at her hair.

'I'll come with you while you have your coffee,' she says.

They walk upstairs to the coffee counter. Howard is so pleased with himself he feels he can say anything.

'Didn't I do that well?' he cries. 'Has anyone *ever* come up to you and introduced himself like that before?'

Howard meets Phil Schaffer in various pubs, down there in the sea of lights – Phil knows the city intimately already – and they walk round for hours, talking and yawning and doing joky things. They go to amusement arcades, and start a poetry magazine, and buy pornographic books, and release long streamers of lavatory paper from the top of the Pan-Am building to see whose will be carried farther by the wind as it falls. Phil makes every dark doorway seem an entrance to a sinister underworld, every advertisement and book title a revelation of the absurd. Their regular promenading grounds are the streets that abound with dirty bookshops and prostitutes and Chinese restaurants. They are both 19 at the time, and if there's anything in the world that's sweeter than being 19 when you're 37, it's being 19 in a street full of whores and dirty bookshops and Chinese restaurants.

As they go about the city they search for God. They know he won't be in any of the obvious places – that wouldn't be his style at all. He won't have his name on the door. He'll be ex-directory, lurking behind some apparently innocent front, like the head of an intelligence agency.

One day they find him. They are looking through the directory board in the foyer of the RCA building, reading aloud to each other all the names of firms they find ridiculous ('How about this? Cock o' the North Erection Co.' 'What?' 'Sorry – Construction Co. Hey, what goes on in this one, though? Toplady and Partners!' 'Disgusting!') when they discover a firm on the sixteenth floor called Geo. Dewey (Optical) Ltd.

Phil whistles, and looks at Howard with raised eyebrows.

'What?' says Howard.

'GDO,' says Phil.

'I don't get it.'

'Anagram.'

'Fantastic!'

They go up to the sixteenth floor at once, not at all sure what they are going to do. But as they hesitate outside the door marked Geo. Dewey (Optical) Ltd, a man comes out. He is wearing a *tweed cap* and an *ancient blue trench-coat*. He has a *slight limp*.

Phil raises his eyebrows in Howard's direction at once.

They spring into the next lift, catch sight of him again in the lobby, and trail him for miles, on underground trains and buses, out into sparse unfinished housing estates among the vague terrains on the outskirts of the city, elaborating increasingly fantastic and boring explanations of his destination and business, until, mercifully, they lose him, and can return to the dirty bookshops and Chinese restaurants.

'Have you ever thought why it gets dark each evening?' asks Phil one day, as they leave one coffee bar where nothing is happening, and walk to another, to find out if anything is happening there.

'What do you mean?' replies Howard. 'The world's turning round!'

'But *why* is the world turning round? Who's turning it?'

'Not . . . Geo. Dewey (Optical) Ltd?'

'Of course. Think what would happen to the electric light industry if it didn't get dark every night. And the entertainments industry. And gambling, and girls. Would you be surprised if I told you that the seven major shareholders in GEC, Westinghouse, Con Edison, NBC, and CBS, are Mr El, Mr Elohim, and Mr Adonai, YHWH Inc., Ehyeh-Asher-Ehyeh, Shaddai Holdings, and

Zebaot International?'

Howard puts a significant look on his face while he thinks. Then some faint memory stirs.

'But aren't they the Seven Names of God?' he asks.

'*Right!* Seven aliases, and he's got the moon and stars sewn up as well!'

Whores, dirty bookshops, Chinese restaurants – and the whole scene manipulated by the invisible wires of this all-powerful secret monopoly!

Fan*tastic*!

'But you *must* know!' says Howard to Felicity, walking up and down the living-room and clutching an amazed hand to his forehead.

'Well, I don't,' says Felicity evenly, peering closely at her sewing.

'They must have told you at school!'

'No.'

'Oh, come on! You're just trying to shock me. You're just trying to amuse me – to set it up for me so that I can walk up and down the room gasping and shouting "I don't believe it!"'

Felicity says nothing.

'And all right,' says Howard, 'I'm enjoying it. I'm having a good time walking up and down here and being astonished that anyone could be so ignorant. It's really made my day, to discover that there's someone in the world who still doesn't know who the seven major shareholders in GEC, Westinghouse, Con Edison, NBC, and CBS are!'

'All right,' says Felicity. 'You've finished enjoying my not knowing. Now you can enjoy telling me.'

One day his father phones. It's eleven years since he died, but Howard recognizes his voice at once, and is able to save him the embarrassment of deciding whether to say, 'This is your father,' or, 'This is Laurence,' or, 'This is your Dad.'

'It's you!' he interrupts deftly.

'That's right,' says his father gratefully. 'It's me.'

'Well, this *is* a surprise,' says Howard.

'Not too early in the morning to ring, I hope?'

'No, no – we're all up.'

'Only I'm never too sure whether you're going to be up or not.'

'Don't worry. We're all up.'

'I just thought I'd phone and find out how you are. It must be getting on for eleven years now since . . .'

'I suppose it must,' interrupts Howard neatly again, to save his father hesitating over, 'since I died', or 'since I passed away.' He knows instinctively that it's not a subject his father would want to talk about.

'And Felicity?' inquires his father. 'And the children? You've got some children, I should imagine, haven't you?'

'Yes, four. They're fine. We're all fine. And you?'

'Oh, quite well, thank you. Yes. Not too bad.'

'And Mother, and Auntie Lou, and Mildred?'

'Oh, we can't complain, all things considered.'

'Good. Good.'

Howard is very moved. Because this is what he always felt after his father died – that if he could just speak to him *now*, he could really open his heart and say everything, without feeling that strange mute on his vocal chords. And here he is, actually doing it!

'It's nice to hear from you,' he says frankly.

'Well, I just thought I'd ring,' says his father. 'I said to your mother, "I'd better just ring him and find out how he's getting on." '

Howard wants to make some huge impulsive gesture to express the naked love he feels.

'Why don't you both come over and have a cup of tea some time?' he suggests. 'Or lunch, perhaps, if that would make getting back easier?'

'Well, one of these days, perhaps. When the weather's a bit warmer.'

'Yes, well, any time. Just give us a little notice, so that we can get the kettle on.'

There is a silence, during which Howard licks his finger and wipes at a mark on the telephone. When he realizes what he is doing he is amazed. Really, it's fantastic! To be able to sit in silence with his father, without any need to make conversation – so relaxed together that he can sit there licking his finger and wiping marks off the telephone!

'You're not just wasting your time here, I take it?' asks his father. 'You're not just lolling around?'

'No, no,' says Howard, smiling to himself, but touched by his father's concern. 'No, I'm rather busy, in fact.'

'You've got a job, have you?'

'Oh, I've got a job all right.'

'Because it would be a very sad thing to waste your opportunities in a place like this.'

'No, no. I've got a job.'

'Only too easy to lounge about all day enjoying yourself, I realize that. But you'd regret it in the long run, I think, wouldn't you? You'd feel you hadn't made the best use of your time here. Let your chances slip through your fingers. You've got to think about the future, you see.'

'No, well, this job's got quite good prospects. Quite

a generous pensions scheme.'

The sheer pleasure of being able to give his father pleasure like this!

'All right, then,' says his father. 'I just thought I'd make sure you were getting on all right. Give my love to Felicity and the children. You did say you'd got children didn't you?'

'That's right. Give my love to Mother, and Auntie Lou, and Mildred.'

As easy as that! After eleven years!

He has in fact got a job, now his father mentions it, and an astonishingly good one, too, for someone in his first year down from university. He is working with Harry Fischer's design group, which is almost certainly the liveliest team in the profession at this particular moment. They all think so, at any rate, though they turn it into a joke. You can tell how lively they are by the fact that they work not in great white north-lit drawing-offices, like the more fashionable and established groups, but in a few cramped rooms on the fourth floor of an Edwardian commercial block, above a tobacconist and an employment agency, mostly looking out on an air-well.

They are designing the Alps.

Each morning the members of the team come straggling into the dark and dusty offices, yawning and inert; and each morning, as coffee is brought round and work gradually gets under way, the little enclosed world comes alive. Harry Fischer comes out of his room in his shirtsleeves, hoisting his braces up with one hand, and holding in the other some letter or Ministry circular which has arrived in the morning post, and which he reads mockingly aloud to evoke their common derision at the obtuseness and bureaucracy of the world outside the office. They all cackle with pleasure at the absurdity of it; then, as soon as Harry has gone back into his room, they all mock *him*, walking back and forth about the room holding imaginary braces and letter, and talking with a German accent. As the day wears on they begin to mock each other, particularly Neil Strachan, the melancholy Presbyterian geologist, who keeps ruling out half their best ideas as bloody tectonic impossibilities, and who can't do a convincing German accent for the life of him. They talk in joke Scottish voices, and act out the scenes of depressive Presbyterian fornication in which they affect to believe Neil's evenings are spent. Jimmy Jessop, the glaciation expert, who is a skilled pickpocket, undoes the back buttons of Neil's braces as they lean over a diagram together, until Neil loses his temper, and chases Jimmy round the office, shouting that he is going to bloody kill him. Then they all settle down for a bit and design some mountains.

Howard laughs more in his first few weeks on Harry's group than he has ever laughed in his life before. He tries to convey the humour to Phil, but Phil looks at him sardonically and talks of other things. Howard also finds with pleasure that he is beginning to speak a language which is incomprehensible to anyone outside the office, even to Phil – schuppen structure, Pennine 'windows', and Dinaride outliers.

Another thing Howard likes about the job is the money.

Not that the salary is all that large. What tickles Howard is the principle of the thing. *Paying* him! Real money! Him! There's something about it that's delectably . . . *grown-up*.

There are other benefits, too, with a responsible adult ring about them. 'My life's insured by the department,' he explains to Felicity, 'so that if anything happens to me you'd get both a lump sum and a regular income. And the pension arrangements are remarkably good. Under the regulations here they're only allowed to pay up to 80% of your salary from a contributory scheme. But they make it up, from a special non-contributory fund, to 100% of the higest salary level you reach.'

'How much will that be?' asks Felicity.

'I haven't the slightest idea,' says Howard. 'It's just the principle of the thing that struck me.'

He saves his monthly salary slips, and his bank statements and cheque stubs, and reads through them all each time he adds another item, entranced by the complex passage of money through his hands.

His intention is to form a complete collection, covering the whole of his working life, so that he will have a real store of memories to look back upon in his old age.

He likes the work itself, too.

He likes the sense of working against limitations, of seeing what kind of mountain shape can be developed given certain unalterable geological and meteorological data. And then the sudden lurching shift of perspective, the falling through the bottom of things, when you discover that these constants have been or could be altered after all.

He likes the way they suddenly drop the whole interlocking tangle of folding and faulting and erosion, and stroll round for lunch in the pub they've adopted.

He likes the smell of dust in the office, and the smell of clean white shirts as the sweat begins to come through the armpits.

He likes the days when nothing seems to happen, and rain runs down the windows, and through somebody else's windows on the other side of the airwell you can see girls with piles of lacquered hair laughing and making sudden small self-conscious movements, as they flirt with young men in Italian-cut suits, silent behind the layers of glass.

He likes the endless consultations and conferences. The reaching for cigarettes from packets open on the table. The sinking of heads upon hands. The sudden impossible inspirations – 'Look, just a minute, why don't we simply scrap the Triassic strata altogether, and to hell with it?' – 'Because that's what's holding up Mont Blanc.' – 'Oh, yes.'

He likes the crises. The afternoon when they discover that they have to have a complete outline plan of the Dolomites ready for the Minister by nine o'clock the following morning, and all stay working into the small hours, until their backs are aching and their eyes closing, and they all love each other and are united in extremity against the entire world. And the other afternoon – crises are always in the afternoon – when Harry, back from an official lunch, comes out of his office and announces, 'Gentlemen, I thought you might be interested to know that the location of the Alps has been shifted to Central Africa.' Lightheaded, laughing despair. Mutinous abandonment of work. Discussion of mass resignation and letters to the papers. Wanderings out to buy shirts and more cigarettes. A holiday atmosphere.

One morning Harry summons Howard into his office. 'Shut the door,' he says. 'Sit down.'

He hoists his braces up, tips his chair back, and begins to sharpen a matchstick into a toothpick. He is in his fatherly mood.

'How long have you been in the office?' he asks. 'Five months,' says Howard.

'How are the moraines coming along?'

'Fine. I've finished the production drawings for three of them now.'

Harry curls up his lip, and picks at his gold-filled teeth with the matchstick. He has given half the designers in the business their start; survived two famous resignations on principle; been in prison and concentration camp; outlived one wife and divorced another.

'Take a rest from moraines for a bit,' he says. 'I'll tell you what I want you to do. I want you to design a trademark for the Alps.'

'A trademark?' says Howard, not understanding. 'How do you mean?'

Harry takes the matchstick out of his mouth and points it at Howard.

'If I knew how I meant I shouldn't be asking you to design it, because that's what design is, knowing how you mean. What I want is something, I don't know what, but when you see it it means the Alps. That's how you stay in front in this business, Howard. You do a good piece of work. Then you put a good big handle on it, so that everyone can get hold of it and pick it up. Go and design me a good big handle, Howard.'

Howard sits tensely at his drawing-board, his mouth tight shut, his eyes gazing unseeing at the paper, rigid with anxiety to produce a good big handle. Impossible ideas crowd through his brain. He tries to follow the line of Harry's thought, but all he can think of is Harry's accent. Harry's accent makes him think of Vienna, and Vienna of E. H. Gombrich. Gombrich makes him think of the readiness with which the eye recognizes the features of the human face. He sketches out a domed mountain with a pair of high corries and ledges that seem to form eyes and eyebrows, and a vertical crest of rock running down between them, passing a snowfield on either side . . . He scribbles the absurdity out. He tries again with a vast seated figure like a Henry Moore, in which a hanging valley forms a kind of lap . . . His mind wanders. He thinks about girls he might meet, and the evolution of the brassière. And then suddenly, for no reason at all, he finds he is thinking of the Pyramids. With a jolt of excitement, as if his heart has stopped for a moment, his mind leaps to the image of a pyramid-shaped mountain. A mountain that weirdly echoes the shape not of the human face but of a human artefact! A mountain that looks as if it was designed by the Ancient Egyptians, instead of by God, and his advisers! Just made dramatically steeper, like this, and then subtly twisted out of alignment, like *that* . . .

An hour-and-a-half later he has finished a rough plan and elevation. It's exactly as he conceived it, except that instead of twisting it he has knocked the top slightly cock-eyed, like the cow with the crumpled horn.

He goes into Harry's office, and without a word puts the drawings on the desk in front of him. For some moments Harry gazes at them in silence, slowly plucking the lefthand strap of his braces away from the shoulder, and letting it snap back against the shirt. Howard can feel the muscles on his face trembling slightly, as they tense for a self-deprecating smile at Harry's appreciation. His head makes little involuntary movements, the first beginnings of the small pleasurable movements which his whole body will make as a kind of modest disclaimer in the face of Harry's approval.

Harry's appreciation is even more whole-hearted than he expects. He begins to laugh. He laughs violently, excitedly, hammering his hand up and down on the desk. People come drifting into the room to see what's up. They look over Harry's shoulder, and slowly begin to smile. They glance up at Howard, looking at him in a new way. 'This your idea?' they ask curiously.

Howard twitches. He runs a hand across his mouth,

as if to keep wiping off his smile. He leans against the wall, and pushes himself off, and leans against it once more. His whole body is full of a genial electric warmth.

In just six-and-a-half hours he has produced the Matterhorn.

It's a real young man's mountain, of course. He never does anything quite so bold again, or quite so fast.

But people in the office regard him differently now. They still mock the slow way he speaks. 'Urm,' they all boom ponderously, on varying notes, when he fails to answer a question at once. They still mock his eagerness, and mimic the keen forward inclination with which he walks, as if he can't wait to get where he is going. But he can see from their eyes that they look upon him now as someone who will transcend the collective and desert it. So he is able to become even more modest than before. He speaks more slowly, leans more eagerly, so as to offer more opportunity to the mimics; smiles more disarmingly at the result. He knows he is behaving well, that his behaviour slots precisely, with a well-oiled click, into the space in the universe that's waiting for it.

Meanwhile the Matterhorn begins to grow famous. Projections of it are reproduced in the papers. It catches people's imagination, and becomes, as Harry wanted, a kind of pictogram to represent the whole range. A newspaper refers to Harry in a headline as 'Mr Matterhorn'.

'I should get your lawyers on to that,' says Jimmy Jessop.

'Not at all,' says Howard. 'He's the head of the de-

66

partment. It was his idea, really.'

They all instantly mimic him, pressing their hands together and casting their eyes soulfully upwards.

'Manifest unto us thy holy arse, O St Harry, that this thy humble servant Howard may lick it,' chants Jimmy.

But they are very fond of him, underneath it all.

One day Harry comes into the office silently holding up an advance copy of one of the professional journals. It contains the first detailed plans for the Himalayas, which all the big names in the business have been working on for years. Everyone in the office comes crowding round, anxious to see the strength of the opposition. Silently they gaze. Silently Harry turns the pages over.

'Well?' demands Harry.

'Well,' says Brian McDermott cautiously, 'they're very *big* . . .'

They all let their breath out in an explosion of laughter. It's true. They're very big, and they're very expensive, and that's about all you can say for them. A prestige job, with not a suggestion of the wit and sinew and quirky humanity that informs the stuff they are turning out in Harry's office. Which means that, unless the Andes group produce any surprises, Harry Fischer's little bunch of boozers are the best bloody mountainbuilders in the world.

Howard would like to put his arms about the whole team, as they crowd round the journal, smelling of shirts, and squeeze them all, and fuse them into one perfect corporate human being.

'You know what the trouble is with these bloody monstrosities?' asks Neil Strachan, turning back the pages of the journal with his disapproving Presbyterian fingers. 'In three bloody words?'

They wait.

'No bloody Matterhorn,' says Neil.

All his friends know that it was Howard who did the Matterhorn, in spite of his modesty, because Prue Chase makes a point of telling everyone.

'You know Howard, don't you?' she says, as she levers him into conversations at parties. 'He did the design for the Matterhorn, though he modestly lets Harry Fischer take all the credit for it.'

Or else she turns to him in the middle of dinner and asks: 'What's happening about the Matterhorn, Howard? They *are* going ahead with it, aren't they? It won't be affected by the credit squeeze . . . ? Shirley, you know it was really Howard who designed it, don't you?'

Prue handles the public relations for all her friends in this way. It's her assiduity which enables them all to be so modest about their success – and they all are pretty successful, one way and another.

Charles Aught is doing terribly well in inspiration, for example.

'The last time we saw you,' Prue says to him, as she ladles the *haricots* around his *gigot*, 'you were just desperately trying to find a second line to go after "Goe, and catch a falling starre." Did you have any luck?'

'Prue, love!' cries Charles Aught, pleased. 'How clever of you to remember! Yes, as a matter of fact I did. "Goe, and catch a falling starre,/Get with child a mandrake roote." '

'Charles, that's *brilliant*!' cries Prue.

'Brilliant!' says Roy, her husband, from the other end of the table.

'I thought that would really zonk him,' says Charles.

'They've put Charles on to inspiring Donne,' explains Prue to the people around the middle of the table, 'because he did so fantastically well with Yeats.'

'Well, either you get on with someone or you *don't*,' says Charles. 'And with John I do. He's really rather a honey. As a matter of fact I usually just give him the first line or two and leave him to get on with it. He's quite literate. Unlike some I've worked with.'

Bill Goody is trying to stop the laws of logic being passed.

'How's your truly heroic battle against the law of Excluded Middle going?' asks Prue. 'You know, Charles, don't you, that the Government's trying to steamroller a law through to say that everything either is the case or isn't the case?'

'Oh, we've done a deal on Excluded Middle,' says Bill. 'We've called our campaign off as a *quid pro quo* for their accepting the need for legislation to control the conservation of energy.'

Simon Winter has raised two people from the dead.

'Are they both all right still?' asks Prue. 'Bill, you know it was Simon who brought those two people back to life.'

'One's popped off again, I'm afraid,' says Simon. 'The other's jogging along all right. Bit brain-damaged, that's all.'

Roy Chase himself is very big in counselling, though Prue out of conjugal modesty always makes his efforts sound ridiculous. 'Poor Roy!' she says. 'The only people who seem to get put through to him are little girls who want ponies for Christmas and wives who want their husbands dead.'

Roy grins.

'More apple crumble, anyone?' he says.

And everyone knows that really he is advising medieval kings and nineteenth-century Prime Ministers.

There's room for them all to do well in this place,

that's the thing. There's plenty of demand for their talents. Because here they are, right at the centre of things, with the whole universe to plan and control and advise and entertain. And they have the satisfaction of knowing that they are indispensable. For what would the universe be without this concentration of moral and intellectual power in the metropolis? Mere chaos. Undifferentiated interstellar gas. Nothing.

And there is room for them all to do better than each other.

'I mean,' says Howard to a girl called Rose he meets at a party, as they sit on the stairs around two in the morning, talking seriously, her dark eyes looking up seriously into his, 'I'm the best mountain-designer *in the universe*. It sounds ridiculous – it *is* ridiculous – it's one of those huge ridiculous facts that one tries to close one's eyes to, they're so absurd – and I'm only mentioning it because it's two o'clock in the morning, and I feel I can say anything to you. And this would be an *insupportable* thing to know about oneself, if one thought that this implied some superiority over the people around one. But in this society it doesn't. Because the people around one are all the best at something else in the universe. Charles Aught has the best working relations with Donne, Roy Chase is the best at helping people, and so on. You might say, what about the other mountain-designers I work with? How can they be best at mountain-designing if I am? And that's a very good question. But the answer is, each one secretly *thinks* he's the best. And the more obvious it is that *I'm* the best, the more convinced they are that under the surface, in some subtler way that only a more discriminating critic would appreciate, *they* are . . . This is what we've achieved by extreme centralization and extreme specialization – a society so complex that everyone in it is winning the race. Do you see what I mean?'

Rose runs her finger slowly round the rim of her glass.

'What about me?' she said. 'What am I best at?'

Howard takes her hand emotionally.

'What you're best at,' he says, 'is sitting here on these particular stairs at this particular hour of the night with that particular way of looking, and then saying 'What am I best at?'

What astonishes Howard, though, is why he should be allowed to be who he is, and live in such a perfectly organized society.

'Why *me?*' he asks Phil Schaffer, as the two of them sit late in Indian restaurants, eating blazing vindaloos after watching old Humphrey Bogart movies at cinemas beyond the railway sidings, on autumn nights when each sodium light has a yellow halo in the foggy air. 'What have I ever done to deserve this?'

'What do you mean?' says Phil shortly (he makes a point of trying to keep Howard's modesty within reasonable bounds). 'You passed the exam to get into the place, didn't you? What do you expect?'

The exam! Of course! Howard has entirely forgotten about it. He came up on the train for a few days, very nervous, wearing his best suit. He remembers sitting on a hard seat, among a hundred other candidates in a large, impressively ancient room, scribbling a General Essay paper for three hours on EITHER Political Necessity OR 'Enrichissez-vous!' not at all sure what the examiners would be looking for in the answers – their ideas or his ideas, or the former subtly disguised as the latter, or the latter masquerading as the former.

In the end he boldly put down his own ideas, without any thought as to whether the examiners would find them palatable or not. He set forth an idealistic view of a society in which all privilege would be done away with, and in which wealth and power would be fairly shared, on the basis of competitive public examinations with General Essay papers on EITHER Natural Justice OR 'Everything is for the best in the best of all possible worlds.'

And passed. So the foundations of his existence in this society are absolutely secure.

———

Phil has an incredibly good job, too. He is creating man.

Or at any rate, he is with one of the research teams working on the man project. Half the university departments and industries in the city are involved. The end-product, as everyone knows from all the projections and mock-ups they keep making public to try to justify the wildly escalating costs, will have two arms and two legs, a language capability, and a fairly sophisticated emotional and moral response. The general idea is to build something pretty much in their own image.

'As a matter of fact,' Phil tells Howard one day, as they walk along the street eating fish and chips out of a Greek newspaper, 'I think it's probably going to be the spitting image of *you*.'

'What?' frowns Howard.

'I sit there in the laboratory,' says Phil, 'trying to think how people go, and I can't remember. Do they really physically raise a sardonic eyebow, and make a long face, or only metaphorically? What expression do they have when they're thinking black thoughts about someone they're trying to ingratiate themselves with, or when they're being praised for qualities they're aware they don't possess? I think of all the people I know, and I can't remember how any of them behave. The only person I can ever think of is you. I always know what *you'd* do. I can always imagine what you'd think, and how you'd look. So bit by bit you're being written into the programme and fed into the computer. I hope you're flattered.'

Howard *is* flattered. But he doesn't like to let Phil see this. So he adopts a humorous ape-like shamble, knees bent and feet turned out.

'Ferkin ell,' he says, in a special humorous artificial voice which he uses from time to time with Phil, to ward off jokes he has not entirely understood.

'I must get that down,' says Phil. 'When told that man is being created in his image, he bends knees, turns feet out, and utters a small trisyllabic croak from the bottom of larynx.'

For Christmas Howard buys his children a complete working model of their family and its life. There, on the playroom floor on Christmas morning, is their house, the children's school, the great towers of the city . . . Switch on and move the appropriate levers on the banks of controllers, and the children come running out of the house, little pink-cheeked creatures half an inch high, who turn to wave at Felicity as she comes out on the terrace to see them off to school. Cars purr back and forth along the expressways, bearing the Bernsteins to dinner with the Chases, the Chases to the Waylands, the Waylands for a Christmas morning drink with the Bakers. And there's Howard himself, three-quarters of an inch high, and a little too freshly complexioned to be true, climbing into his car, running upstairs to his office, ushering Felicity through lighted front doors, shaking hands, kissing cheeks . . .

The children play with it for half an hour, then run outside with their new toboggan instead. But Howard can't tear himself away from it. Late that night, after the children have finally gone to bed, Felicity finds him lying full-length on the playroom floor once again, still absorbed.

'Look,' he says, 'here are the Waylands coming up the Parkway to call on Charles Aught . . . There *you* are, taking the children out to tea with Ann Keat . . .'

He glances up and sees her expression.

'Sorry,' he says. 'I'm just coming. But you can actually see it all! That's what gets me about it. You can really get hold of it all. And it all does work, that's the amazing thing. It all does in fact make sense.'

'I suppose so. But doesn't it get rather boring after a bit?'

He moves some more levers, thinking about this. The children come running home from school. The Kessels pick up the Chases, and drive into town to go to the theatre.

'I think perhaps that's what I like most of all about it,' he says.

A great joke – Howard and Felicity are invited to a reception at the Palace!

Howard sits at the breakfast table with the card in his hand, giggling over it.

'You'll have to buy a hat!' he says.

'What?' says Felicity, astonished. 'You're not thinking of going?'

'Of course!' says Howard. 'Why not? We're scarcely going to feel we've sold our souls for a plate of strawberries and cream, are we?'

'You'll have to rent a morning suit. You realize that?'

'Sure. It'll be an absolute riot. I'll go in being about fifty, with grizzled hair and a rather lined face.'

'I don't want to be fifty!'

'No, you be thirty-five, and rather sunburnt. We'll cut a real swathe through them. It'll be a hoot.'

A hoot it is, too. Several thousand people standing about in a series of large rooms surrounded by mirrors, so that the entire world appears to be peopled with morning suits and ladies' hats sipping champagne. A band plays selections from *Fiddler on the Roof*. Howard and Felicity move slowly about with their champagne, like everybody else, trying to look as if they are heading somewhere purposeful, and quietly making little humorous comments on the proceedings to each other as they go .'Hello!' squeaks one of the ladies' hats suddenly – and there are the Bernsteins.

'Thank heavens!' cries Felicity.

'It was worth coming just for the relief of finding you here,' says Jack Bernstein.

'Isn't it ghastly?' murmurs Howard.

'Isn't it just?' squeaks Miriam Bernstein.

'It's exactly like a Jewish wedding,' says Jack, 'except they've forgotten to invite Uncle Hymie and Auntie Rae, the ones who never made it.'

They gaze round over each other's shoulders, very pleased with themselves.

'It's fantastic when you think that a lot of people reckon this whole society's evil top to bottom,' says Jack.

Howard laughs.

'No, seriously,' says Jack.

Howard's laughter fades uncomprehendingly away. 'How do you mean?' he says.

'Oh,' says Miriam, 'Jack met some rather hairy young man at a party, that's all.'

'He told me that half the bacteria I'm developing are lethal,' says Jack. 'Going to kill people off like flies.'

'No!' cries Felicity.

'Yes!' squeaks Miriam. 'He said Jack was just part of the system!'

'System?' demanded Howard, looking from one to the other, not understanding any of this. 'What system?'

'Don't you know?' says Miriam dramatically. 'We're all together in a gigantic conspiracy to dominate the world!'

Howard looks round the room, half-believing for a moment that the game he and Phil used to play might be coming to life after all. But at the sight of all those senior conspirators standing uncomfortably around in rented tailcoats he can't help laughing.

'The whole set-up's a *joke*!' he whispers.

'It's an awfully long joke,' says Miriam. 'What I want to know is where God's supposed to be.'

They thread their way among the morning suits, looking. There's a crush over by the door in one of the rooms, with flashbulbs going off every few seconds, but it's impossible to get near enough to see.

'I've half a mind to take off, and have a look from the ceiling,' whispers Howard.

'Go on, then,' urges Miriam.

'We ought to,' says Jack. 'What's the use of being able to fly if you never use it?'

'Up you go,' says Felicity.

They hesitate.

'Supposing *everyone* started doing it?' says Howard.

'I'd do it if I were younger,' says Jack.

'Oh, so would I. Like a shot.'

'I wouldn't give a damn what anyone thought.'

'Jack's put on ten years specially,' explains Miriam.

'So's Howard,' says Felicity. 'But they could be eighteen for a few moments. No one would notice.'

Howard and Jack look at each other.

'I'd feel a fool, frankly, being eighteen in a morning suit,' says Jack.

So they never see God at all.

'Well?' Bill Goody asks Howard at the Chases next day. 'What was he like? Irresistable, was he? Called you Howard and knew all about the Matterhorn?'

'We never saw him,' says Howard.

The remark is a great success. Everyone laughs and bangs on the table.

'Only Howard Baker could manage to be in the same room as God and not to notice him!' cries Rayner Keat.

'The Bernsteins didn't see him either!' protests Howard.

But on second thoughts he erases the remark, and replaces it with a slight smile.

'You didn't *see* God?' cries Phil Schaffer in exasperation, when Howard smilingly repeats his successful remark to him. 'Why are you messing around trying to *see* him? Why don't you *be* God? You can do anything you like here! Don't you understand that yet? You're free! You control your own destiny!'

'No rush,' says Howard wisely. 'There's plenty of time to do everything. I'm going to take it steadily, step by step, and enjoy each step.'

But what's Charles Aught up to? What strange discontent has gone into him? He seems to have been meeting extremists at parties, as well.

Howard's always found him slightly unsettling, it's true. It's something about the contest between his appearance and his manner. He looks like a rather reliable young man who remembers his aunts' birthdays, with his thick roll-neck sweaters and his glowing complexion and mild blue eyes. His eyes gaze steadfastly into yours as you talk. Too steadfastly, seeing too much of you. His voice is soothing. Too soothing, setting you too much at your ease. He knows slightly too many people who happen to be rich.

And there's some nihilistic glint in the depths of those blue eyes.

He invites Howard to lunch one day (sandwiches, in

the garden of a pub down by the river, at a battered green table with a hole in the middle for an umbrella). He wants to talk about getting some of his poets to work on the Alps – he's looking after one or two of the Romantics for a few months, while a colleague of his is sitting on a commission of inquiry.

'They seem to have rather a thing about, I don't know, *nature*,' he tells Howard. 'I thought if we could get their nature thing together with your Alps thing, we might both do ourselves a bit of good. What's the *angle*, do you think? (He said in his film producer's voice.) What could I tempt them with?'

'Well,' says Howard, 'I think they might be quite interested in the way we're bringing up great sedimentary land masses from the south, and driving them up and over the geosynclinal rocks in their path.'

Charles makes a face.

'I don't think most of these loves would know a sedimentary land mass from a steak-and-kidney pudding,' he says. 'Cottages with roses round the door are more their line. And waterfalls. A little bit of sex slipped in somewhere, if at all possible. Could we get a little discreet sexual interest in, do you think? Chaste virgins of the snow, waiting to be ravished? Great icy tits sticking up into the sky? Or how about this? "O Jungfrau, hear my piteous cries/As I ascend thy snow-white thighs." '

'Well . . .' says Howard, smiling awkwardly down into his beer. He hates this kind of talk.

'Oh dear,' cries Charles, gazing at Howard with a concerned look. 'I've said the wrong thing. I've upset you.'

'No, no . . .' smiles Howard.

'I can see you've got some deep unspoken faith in poets. Unacknowledged legislators, and all that.'

'No . . . well . . .'

'I'm afraid you get a bit cynical when you're actually

79

dealing with them. Most of them are in it just for the bylines and the booze, you know. They use the handouts you give them – but half the time they put some snide twist on the story. And one doesn't expect thanks, of course, but when they use the handout – and then turn round and start blaspheming, you really do want to chuck the whole business up, and go and become a monk, or something.'

'Well . . .' says Howard. It's true – he does have some sneaking faith in poets as being fundamentally decent people. He has some kind of innocence which Charles has lost.

'I mean,' he says, 'I suppose I think that writers do a . . . well . . . a pretty good job, really. It can't be all that easy – I mean, if you've ever tried to write anything yourself . . . and often they're badly paid . . . and so on . . .'

Charles stops looking at Howard. He looks down at the table, smiling, and draws a face by running his finger through a ring of beer.

'Oh, sure,' he says gently. 'Admirable sentiments. Lovely thoughts.'

'No, I mean,' says Howard, waving his arms about, 'I mean, isn't it perhaps just that the writers you deal with sort of *live down* to sort of *your expectations*? Don't they behave badly just because they sort of feel that you, that we, sort of make use of them, sort of exploit them?'

'Ah,' murmurs Charles smoothly, 'what would we all do without your idealism?'

Howard feels very strange. It's as if he has been drawn outside himself by indignations; transcended himself; literally risen into the air above his own head, so that he can see beyond the confines of his own life. He sees clearly how things stand, and the words come to him with which to describe them.

'It's not a question of idealism,' he says. 'It's just a

practical, a practical, a practical thing, a thing of sort of, well, here we are, we've got into this place, and we've got a certain, a certain, a, a, a certain job to do. We've got to sort of *create the world*, and so forth, and sort of run it, and so on, and, well, try to make some kind of, of, of sort of *viable proposition* of it, and all the rest of it, and it just seems to me that we can get *better results* if we treat the, if we treat the sort of, well, for want of a better word, the *local inhabitants* with a certain amount of, of, of *respect* and, and, and *trust*, and, and, if we *help* them, and, and *guide* them, to the point where they can become sort of *independent* and sort of self-governing, within the framework of the free, well, of the free, sort of, well, of the, yes, *free* kind of system that we enjoy ourselves.'

He moves heavily about in his chair, frowning, and fiddling with his glass of beer. It slips out his fingers and turns over. A stream of beer runs across the table and drips on to his trouser leg. He feels priggish and preposterous.

And in the right.

––––––––––––

Charles draws another face in beer. The face is smiling a tiny smile.

'At least I don't go round killing the poor buggers,' he says.

Howard looks up at him sharply.

'What do you mean?' he demands. '*Killing* them? Who's killing them?'

'Well, you are.'

'What *are* you talking about?'

'Aren't you?'

'*Killing* people?'

'Well, I don't know,' says Charles, 'but I met this girl in television the other evening, and she said people are going to be dropping off your Matterhorn thing like fleas off a dog.'

For a moment Howard gapes at him, unable to grasp the enormity of the misunderstanding.

'According to this girl,' says Charles, 'great avalanches are going to come sliding down the mountains, burying people by the dozen.'

A great gasping laugh bursts out of Howard.

'This is *fantastic*!' he shouts. 'No one's going to go *up* the mountains! No one's going to go *near* them! Why on earth should they want to? There's nothing but snow and ice and rock up there!'

To soldier doggedly on in the right – and then to crown the campaign with such a clear-cut black-and-white knockdown victory in argument! A sense of exhilaration sweeps through him.

'Well,' says Charles, the lumpish one now, 'that's what this girl told me.'

A delicately ludicrous picture comes into Howard's mind of an enthusiastic little hiker with a rucksack on his back, trying to walk up the side of the Materhorn, and tumbling back with an astonished look on his face.

Howard can't stop himself laughing. He hides his face in his hands.

'I'm sorry,' he says. 'It's rude of me, but . . .'

But he has to behave a little badly. To be in the right – and right about it! It's a pleasure too sweet to be enjoyed without a little sharpness in it.

But when Howard thinks seriously about the kind of rumours that are being spread around, he sees that it really isn't funny. It's terrible that the society they live in should be undermined like that. He feels real anger running in his veins – a generous fury that honourable people should be so traduced.

'I don't care for myself,' he tells Felicity, walking up and down the kitchen as she prepares dinner. 'But it's so unfair on people like Harry Fischer. His whole life's work twisted against him in one poisonous little rumour. And how about Jack? Where would the world be without bacteria? I mean, we all know the world's not *perfect*. But we're all doing our best to *help* people. Providing them with decent mountains to look at, and bacteria to, to, to make cheese with.'

He walks back and forth, transported with outrage.

'It's so unfair on *you*,' he says, with a broad gesture.

'Me?' says Felicity.

'When I think of all the hours you spend trying to help people with their problems . . .'

For Felicity does voluntary social work, like everybody's wife.

'Oh . . .' she shrugs.

'No, come on!' says Howard. 'Don't let yourself be put down like this! Hours you spend on that phone, listening to people pour out their problems!'

'Yes,' says Felicity doubtfully. 'But I'm not sure I actually *help* them very much . . .'

'Well, you *listen* to them!'

'Oh, I *listen* to them. But . . .'

'But that's what they *need*! You listen – and you case-work them.'

'What most of them need is money, more than anything else,' she says.

'Oh, sure!' cries Howard, his heart full of love for her. 'And there'd be nothing easier than popping a cheque in the post to them, or sending them some cast-off woollies, or ladling some soup into them, or offering them advice. But you're too good at your job to give in to that kind of temptation. You know they've got to learn to confront their own problems, and work out their own solutions.'

'Well . . .' says Felicity.

'No, you keep quiet! I'm not having you running yourself down all the time! So – you listen in silence; and you casework them; and you set up case-conferences about them; and you refer them to other agencies; and you work up your notes on case-handling for the journals.'

Howard stops walking up and down, and looks out of the window. He has just seen that the ultimate aim of the caseworker must not be to casework at all, but to get his cases to face up to caseworking themselves. He has a vision of the caseworker as becoming increasingly abstract, first not commenting, then not even uttering sympathetic noises, finally not even listening; merely a benign presence disposing to good.

Howard is becoming something of an expert on the theory of social work, in fact; Rose is doing it, too. She never *stops* doing it. She's always nervously brushing the hair out of her eyes and saying that she can't come out with Howard because she has to go and see a client.

'To hell with the client,' says Howard, catching her

hand and smiling at her. (They are standing on some windy street corner, say.)

'No, I have to,' says Rose, taking her hand away and frowning.

He catches her other hand.

'He's appearing in court tomorrow,' she says. 'Honest.'

'Which one's this?' asks Howard, taking a strand of her hair and wrapping it round his finger. 'The one who chopped up his wife and married her sister? Or is this the lady with the subnormal twins by her paternal grandfather?'

'I hate your making a joke of it,' says Rose, pulling her hair away.

Howard makes a series of appalling little kissing noises.

'It's someone who's lost his job,' says Rose, 'and he hasn't got anywhere to live.'

He leans forward and kisses her cheek. She leans her elbow against his shoulder, and her head on her fist, and inspects his face from a distance of twelve inches, frowning. (They're sitting at the corner of a teashop table, say.) She runs her finger slowly along his chin, as if inspecting it for dust.

'He's nowhere to sleep tonight,' she says.

'How terrible!' says Howard, brushing his knuckles gently against her eyebrows.

'It *is* terrible.'

'Ghastly.'

'I must ring round and . . .'

He kisses her lips.

'This isn't right,' she says.

'No . . .'

'We're behaving badly.'

'Yes . . .'

The intimately invading pressure of another body against one's own, from neck down to knees! (Because they are standing just inside the door of her room, say.)

'But this really *is* bad,' she says. 'When my client has nowhere to . . . and other people are . . .'

Heaping handfuls of flesh; scooping handfuls of each other, seized libidinously just anywhere, just anyhow! (Because they are stumbling backwards over a precipitation of hasty, inside-out clothes, say.)

'Wouldn't it be terrible to be bad?' he says to her right hip. 'You'd never know what a relief it was to stop being good.'

'Great,' says Phil. 'This is very helpful. Keep going.'

'Well, I simply *laughed* at him,' says Howard. 'I said to him, "But no one's going to go *up* the mountains! No one's going within ten miles of them!"'

Howard is telling Phil about his conversation with Charles Aught. Phil is making notes on it for his Man programme.

'God, it's handy having you around!' says Phil, scribbling as fast as he can. 'This is just the kind of thing you waste months reconstructing under laboratory conditions – the difference in reaction between when you think you're morally right, and when you think you're factually right. So let me just check. First you laughed at him?'

'That's right.'

'How?'

'Oh, a sort of astonished laugh. Ha-*ha*! Something like that.'

'And then you said: "But no one's going to go up the mountains!" Just like that? No repetitions? No sort-ofs?'

'I don't think so.'

86

'This is a most astonishing contrast with the moral response, you see. Only a minute or two earlier you were saying things like: "It's just a sort of a, a sort of a, a, a, a question of as it were sort of behaving sort of, well, for want of a better word, decently, sort of thing." And now here you are getting out one, two, three . . . nine words in a row without any defensive byplay at all.'

'Exactly. But we had got on to a subject I do happen to know something about. I don't know much about most things, but I do know whether people will be going up the Alps or not.'

Phil makes a note.

'May I just ask you one more question?' he says.

'Shoot.'

'Just say if you'd prefer to knock off.'

'No, no. It really gives me a kick to be of some use like this.'

'Well,' says Phil, 'do you remember that time when we were undergraduates, and we hitch-hiked to Rome?'

'Yes,' says Howard, puzzled. 'But what's that got to do with it?'

'And on the way we went through Switzerland?'

'Yes. But . . .'

'And in the youth hostel in Interlaken we met an American called Todd?'

Howard thinks.

'The man with the beard?' he asks.

'That's right,' says Phil. 'A curly black beard.'

'The one who used to hollow out the inside of a baguette for breakfast, and fill it up with condensed milk, and lower it into his mouth like a sword-swallower?'

'That's right.'

Howard laughs. 'That was the lunatic who insisted we climbed the Eiger with him,' he says. 'And the clouds came down, and we lost the path, and we almost walked over the top of a thousand-metre cliff, and . . .'

His voice trails away. The smile fades from his face. He gazes thoughtfully at a spot about halfway up the wall, blinking slowly.

Phil makes rapid notes.

'Good,' he says. 'Well done. That's nice. I like the blinking. I shouldn't have thought of the blinking.'

Howard has the feeling that the floor is dropping away beneath his feet, as if he is in an express lift.

His voice sounds as if it is attempting to name the floors as he passes them.

'Oh, I see . . .' he says. 'Oh, heavens, I don't think that's got anything to do with it . . . I mean, we only got halfway up . . . The fact that three halfwits without even a rope tried to . . . Well, all right, everyone knows that there are going to be a few fools who insist on trying to break their necks . . . You're always going to get some tiny minority you can't take into considera- tion . . .'

Phil notes it all down.

Howard falls and falls. It's the kind of sensation that people pay money to suffer in fairgrounds. To think that this abyss of revelation was waiting inside himself all the time!

'I see what you mean,' he says at last. He makes little humorous concessive noises in his throat, to admit his mistake. He adopts his familiar ape walk, with knees bent outwards and fingers trailing, to express his wry awareness of having boobed. He is at his most Howard- like, his funniest and most lovable. You can create a good impression on yourself by being right, he realizes, but for creating a good impression on others there's nothing to beat being totally and catastrophically wrong.

Even Phil, noting the syndrome down, can't help smiling a little.

'But what I don't understand,' says Howard later, with genuine humility, 'is how you know more about *everything* than I do. Not only about the city, but about myself, even.'

'Oh, plenty of people know things,' says Phil, and sighs. 'It's the skill *you've* got that really counts – the ability *not* to know things, or to know them without knowing that you know them. If we can get man set up the same way we'll have a real world-beater on our hands.'

'Obviously,' says Howard seriously, 'I shall have to get out of mountains. I can't go on working on instruments of mass destruction.'

Quietly, unhesitatingly – just like that – he faces up to the moral consequences of his realization. In that moment he changes careers – changes lives.

'What are you going to do instead?' asks Phil, chewing up little pieces of graph paper into sodden balls, and flicking them at the laboratory ceiling with a slide-rule to try and make them stick.

'I suppose I'll go into rivers,' says Howard.

'Rivers drown people.'

'Or forests.'

'Forests fall on people.'

'I don't know. Plains, perhaps. I'll have to think about it.'

'Howard,' says Phil, grinning. 'I don't think you've got the point. There isn't *anything* that isn't going to cause trouble. Make the whole world as smooth as a billiard ball, and people are still going to fall over and split their skulls open. Fill the world with nothing but good clean pure air and someone's going to get up into it and fall out of it. I can tell you, the people we're putting together on my project are going to drop to pieces without doing *anything*. They'll sit in their armchairs safely watching television and smiling at the children, and be eaten away by growths and shot in the heart by the disintegration of their own arteries.'

Howard stares at him.

'You're joking, of course,' he says.

'No.'

'But this is terrible!'

'Yes.'

'What job *can* I do, then?'

'You could try doing nothing,' says Phil. 'We could all try doing nothing.'

'Nothing? How do you mean, nothing?'

'Not create the world.'

Howard tries to focus his mind on this idea.

'We couldn't do that,' he says.

'Why not?' says Phil. 'Why don't we leave everything as a nice quiet lot of nothingness?'

'Because obviously . . .' says Howard. 'Because . . . Well, because . . .'

'Because,' says Phil, 'if we didn't have a universe to create and run, and a nice lot of trouble to sort out, there wouldn't be any point to our existence. The whole thing's a gigantic boondoggle.'

'Oh, for heaven's sake!' says Howard.

'Exactly,' says Phil.

'The world's not perfect – all right. We're responsible for some of its troubles – all right. We're all profiting from its trouble – *all right!* But that's not to say that we're not doing a reasonably good job *on the whole!* After all, we're the ones who've provided them with . . . I don't know . . . fresh air to breathe, and . . . sunsets to look at, and . . .'

'The soft refreshing rain?'

'Right! And on the whole they're very grateful to us! They're very pleased with what we've done for them!'

'Are they?'

'Of course they are!'

'Has anyone ever bothered to find out? Has anyone ever actually gone over there and had a look at them? Asked them what they felt?'

Howard gazes out of the window of Phil's laboratory, thinking. With natural neatness a new career is opening up to replace the old.

At the airport planes of astonishingly different sizes – like children's toys on different scales mixed up in the same game – queue to use the runway for take-off. They are bound for Brazzaville, Tucson, Irkutsk, Belfast,

London, and Caracas. They wait in the sunshine, trembling slightly, shimmering like mirages in each other's jetstreams, while incoming planes land, from Fairbanks, Bucharest, Huntsville, Glasgow, Karachi, and Albuquerque.

Coming and going, at a cost of 16.450,00 and 34.200,00 and 112.000,00 per person, are cargoes of men in lightweight non-iron suits, and women with carefully underlined eyes and neat pairs of knees. They are examining the world's bauxite reserves, investigating the potentialities of Gabon as a market for learning machines, using their influence to secure the release of political prisoners, setting up conferences to standardize labour law and regulations for the contraceptive pills. They are maintaining contact with the world.

Aboard the plane bound for London, and wearing a pale grey lightweight non-iron suit, with pale blue shirt and striped silk tie, is Howard.

'I've got a research grant,' he explains to the man sitting next to him, who is wearing a dark grey lightweight non-iron suit, with a pale pink shirt and polka-dotted silk tie, as they at last climb out through the heat haze, and undo their seat belts. 'It's a kind of travelling fellowship, really. There are certain aspects of our involvement in the developing world which I feel need looking at. Is our aid getting through to where it's most needed? Is it producing a client mentality? Are we managing to do any good?'

'High time someone started asking a few awkward questions,' says his neighbour, who turns out to be an expert in Moral Law. 'Because they all hate us, you know. Never a word of thanks from any of them for all we've done. I honestly can't see why we bother.'

'No . . . well . . .' says Howard tactfully. 'I think there is a real problem in mutual communication here.'

'England, you're looking at, are you?'

'I thought that would be as good a place to start as

any. I speak the language, you see.'

'Do you? Good God.'

'Oh, I used to live there.'

'I can't stand the people, myself,' says the moral lawyer. 'Feckless lot of layabouts. Dishonest. Dirty. And too big for their boots, on top of everything else. There's some very reasonable golf and fishing, though, if you know where to look for it. And the local woollens are good value. I always try to bring back a sweater for my wife, something like that.'

'I'm quite looking forward to seeing the place again,' says Howard, politely but firmly. He wonders how many of his fellow-countrymen visit Britain with this kind of attitude, undoing all the good work the rest of them are struggling to do. He ostentatiously orders a can of Worthington with his lunch, to show where his sympathies lie.

As they approach London they let down through the shining white floor of cloud into a dull grey light. Drops of rain run back across the windows, almost horizontally.

He had forgotten how small London is. As the car which has been sent for him comes in along the odd little elevated motorway, only four lanes wide, most of the city seems to be below eye-level. Later they wait at fussy complications of traffic-lights. Dumpy Chinese girls walk past along the pavement carrying umbrellas and bags of washing. Elderly ladies with maroon hats fitting closely over tight grey curls turn slowly, dragging their sticks, to look at people who have passed by minutes before.

'I used to live in London,' Howard tells the driver, smiling.

'Oh, yes?' says the driver. He is wearing a faded navy-blue trench-coat with a collar that curls shrunkenly upwards. It looks like a school-child's coat. His sandy hair is brushed straight back over his head, but then turns up a little at the ends, echoing the collar.

'I loved it,' says Howard. 'Never wanted to leave.'

'Oh, well,' says the driver.

Howard struggles to suppress a sense of nothingness, of total unreality.

Things are pretty bad in Britain, Howard soon discovers, as he goes about questioning government officials. Phil was right – people are dying of everything, breaking their necks on level ground, and falling out of clean, empty air. Cancer is endemic. Heart disease is raging, as are arteriosclerosis and various lethal cerebrovascular conditions.

He remembers vaguely about all this from when he was living in the country. But then it seemed somehow natural and inevitable. There is a kind of fatalism in the atmosphere of this place which the officials he meets all seem to share. After his first horrified reaction has passed, Howard begins to think that this fatalism may be the only thing that keeps people sane.

'I see 97,307 people died last year of acute myocardial infarctions,' he remarks to an official in the Department of Health, trying to keep his tone conversational, as they go through the tables of statistics together. He watches the man closely to see how he reacts when he has to talk about this appalling figure.

But he shows no signs of any reaction at all.

'I think that's about average for Western Europe, isn't it?' he says. 'Shall I ask them to send some coffee in?'

He's a decent sort of man – Howard knows his type well from his stay in the country. But while Howard sits there, trying not to think about those 97,000 piled corpses, *he* apparently sits there thinking about coffee.

'4260 people died of aortic aneurysms (non-syphilitic),' Howard reads out. '2335 of nephritis and nephrosis . . . Don't you find these figures at all *disturbing*?'

'Oh, don't run away with the impression that we're not concerned,' says the official defensively. 'We're doing quite a lot of research in most of these areas – though of course we all agree we ought to do more. And we have started putting health warnings on cigarette packets.'

Howard is touched and embarrassed. Not only is the official not complaining of the handicaps with which they have been saddled by Howard's fellow-countrymen – he's *apologizing* that they haven't overcome them!

But what people in general feel about the situation Howard finds it very difficult to determine. A minority kill themselves, or systematically intoxicate themselves, or withdraw into various psychotic or schizophrenic states; but, as the various experts he talks to point out, this is often because of the difficulties they have caused themselves, or been caused by others. He is shown polls indicating percentage satisfaction with the Prime Minister and the performance of the Government. But no one seems to have any figures for the percentage of people who are satisfied with life in general.

'It seems a curious omission,' he murmurs politely. 'It's a rather obvious question.'

The officials and experts all spread their arms helplessly, and give little laughs. Their insouciance is irritating, and also rather charming. But then they don't even seem to have wondered before what they themselves feel about the matter.

'Am *I* happy?' they repeat, visibly embarrassed. 'What, personally? Well . . . yes, I suppose so . . . Reasonably satisfying job, and so on . . . home . . . children . . . I can't really complain . . .'

Howard gazes out of the window of his official car at people in the streets, trying to read the expression on their faces as they wait for buses or try to cross the road. They don't *appear* to be thinking about their sclerosis. They seem to be a simple, happy-go-lucky folk who are content if they can merely catch a bus or two each day, and find a bit of a gap in the traffic to nip through, and survive till bedtime.

'Cheer up!' says his driver, with the curling trench-coat, looking at him in the mirror.

'What?' says Howard.

'That look on your face! Don't worry – it may never happen. That's my philosophy.'

Howard does his best to smile. Under the long curling hair hanging lankly over the driver's neck, Howard has noticed, is a tumour the size of a sparrow's egg.

He arranges a meeting with a leading dissident intellectual, J. G. D. McKechnie, to get another perspective on the problem. It takes place in McKechnie's flat in Belsize Park. They sit in flowered armchairs in front of the gas-fire, and drink Nescafé out of flowered mugs.

What J. G. D. McKechnie says explains a lot.

It's a question of profit, he explains. The whole complex. There is massive investment in disease and mortality which the system protects by distracting people's attention from it. It has a vested interest in brainwashing people into believing that they are happy, when in fact they are not and could not possibly be. It does this by drugging them with things which it persuades them to believe they want. McKechnie lists specifically food, drink, sex, attractive clothing; labour-saving machines and mechanical transport; holidays and leisure activities; so-called 'high' culture – music, art, literature, etc. – and so-called 'pop' culture – in which he includes the singing of old Tin Pan Alley songs, such as 'Show Me the Way to Go Home', in public houses run by the big breweries.

'Winter sports?' asks Howard, thinking uncomfortably of the Alps.

'Right,' says J. G. D. McKechnie.

'Walking tours in the Tyrol?'

'All that kind of shit.'

So this explains his driver's attitude. This explains the neutral look on the faces of people in the streets. And perhaps even the look on J. G. D. McKechnie's face.

'What about you?' Howard asks him sympathetically. 'Are *you* happy?'

McKechnie seems surprised by the question. He frowns, and curls his beard round his fingers, gazing about the room. A Siamese cat picks its way among the confusion of London Library volumes lying open on the table. At the window overlooking the garden the young girl with whom he is living sits painting – tiny brush strokes, with her head very close to the work, silent, absorbed. A clock chimes the quarter.

'Oh, sure,' he said, sliding down into his armchair and putting his feet on the bookcase – he is not wearing socks, Howard notices. '*I'm* perfectly happy. Don't try and make *me* out to be some kind of embittered nut compensating for an unsatisfactory sex-life.'

So McKechnie was right. Even *he* has been drugged by the system and anaesthetized against the perception of his own misery. His jaws have been wrenched open, like everyone else's, and the tranquillizers crammed in – a Siamese cat, a few books and records, an eighteen-year-old girl with wild hair and intent lips slightly parted . . .

Howard's heart goes out to him. They must start the world again, to produce a McKechnie who is freed from cat, books, records, and girl.

———————

Michael Wayland's over in London, too.

There is a familiar roaring noise as Howard is crossing the lobby of the Connaught, and there is this compelling figure bearing down upon him, pinioning his arms, and searching his face with eager recognition.

'Michael!' cries Howard, astonished.

'   !' grimaces Michael eloquently, no less astonished.

'Howard,' Howard reminds him.

'Howard,' agrees Michael.

'What on earth are you doing over here?'

'The usual thing,' says Michael. 'Reading out various grim warnings on the Autocue to the natives about the way things are going. Trying to put the fear of God into them. And you?'

'Oh,' says Howard wittily, 'trying to get the fear of God out of them.'

'Do you think the bar's open?' says Michael. 'Let's go and have a drink. I can't tell you how pleased I am to see you! I thought I was in for another evening of getting slightly drunk on my own.'

They get slightly drunk together, in a most agreeable way, and then wander round the West End, making jokes about the photographs outside the strip clubs. They are very pleased with each other's company – as pleased as only two fellow-countrymen meeting each other in a strange city can be.

'Lord, this city's a dump!' says Michael.

'Oh, I don't know,' says Howard, trying to be reasonable.

'No, it's the last place God made. I can't imagine how we all put up with living here.'

'I quite enjoy watching all the people go by,' says Howard, 'and wondering what's going on inside their heads.'

'But that's you all over, Howard. You always manage to find some good in people. I can't stand them. For a start they smell.'

'Well . . .'

'Oh, come on. Be honest.'

'They smell different, that's all.'

'They smell, Howard. They're rude and indifferent, and when they're not being rude and indifferent they're licking your boots and telling you what they think you want to hear.'

'Michael, I think a lot of this is really *our* fault . . .'

'Oh, bollocks! Don't let them give you that line. They're born whiners.'

'No, Michael, I honestly think it's the result of the system that we're part of . . .'

'Don't believe a word they tell you, Howard. They're all liars. They're all on the cadge.'

'I must admit,' concedes Howard, 'the telephone service is a bit erratic. And the hotel's lost my laundry.'

'I'll tell you what gets me,' says Michael. 'Having to be so careful all the time not to offend their susceptibilities. Though what right this lot have got to have susceptibilities I can't imagine. Don't you find, about five o'clock each day, that you've got a polite smile permanently creased into your face, like rigor mortis?'

'I know what you mean,' says Howard. 'But . . .'

'Mind!' cries Michael, and steers Howard round a little heap of excrement in the middle of the pavement. Howard can't help laughing. Michael enacts a scene where, smiling politely, he attempts to use a telephone to inform some touchy British official that here is a heap of something untoward lying on one of his pavements. Passers-by step into the gutter and try not to look at them as they both lean against walls and shop-fronts, laughing helplessly.

'No, but seriously,' says Howard. 'They do have a terrible life.'

'They have a terrible life,' says Michael, growing serious as well, 'because a terrible life is what these people understand. A terrible life is what these people *enjoy*. There's nothing they love more than an interesting little family tragedy, or a nice little disease to muck themselves up with.'

Howard continues to protest. But secretly he knows that Michael is right. There *is* something curiously unappetizing about these people. Even McKechnie. Especially McKechnie. It gives Howard an extraordinary sense of personal liberation to admit this to himself. There is something very sweet about strolling through the streets of London with a fellow-countryman, and in the privacy afforded by their shining armour of courtesy and concern, to frankly recognize the difficult truth : that they are better than the people around them.

'It's some friend of yours who's responsible for man, isn't it?' asks Michael, looking sideways at Howard.

'Phil Schaffer. Well, he's one of the design team.'

'Making rather a pig's eye of it, isn't he?'

'Oh, I wouldn't say that,' says Howard loyally. 'I

think it's a remarkable achievement. On the whole.'

His loyalty to Phil sets his blood circulating with a pleasant warmth. So does the discovery that Phil needs his loyalty. It's very agreeable to be able to reach down and offer someone a helping hand – particularly someone he has looked up to for so long.

Later they meet up with a couple of girls whose telephone numbers Michael finds in his pocket, and as a crazy night out they all have dinner at the Ritz.

'But seriously,' cries Howard to Michael in a dramatic voice, over the coffee and brandy, waving his cigar about, 'what are we going to *do* about these people? How can we solve the problem?'

The girls both stare at him, obviously impressed by the scale and force of his concern. They are all a little drunk.

'Keep killing them,' says Michael humorously, resting a hand on each girl's forearm. 'Wheel on the cholera. The more we keep them down, the less of them there'll be to get themselves into trouble.'

'Oh, charming,' says one of the girls.

'Have another chocolate, love,' Michael invites her, smilingly holding out the dish. 'Get a little more refined sugar into your arteries.'

Howard's report on the human condition, when it finally appears, is a remarkably balanced and perceptive document. He resolutely refuses to give way to the temptation to blame the local inhabitants for their problems. He points out that many of the characteristics of man which outsiders find distasteful reflect genuine local needs and aspirations.

He recognizes that there is a real divergence of expert opinion between those who believe that men are happy because they are miserable, and those who believe that men are miserable because they are happy; and wisely arrives at a synthesis of both views.

He cautions against any hasty attempts at imposing reform from outside, warning that they would be very likely to upset the delicate social and economic balance which society has achieved – to cause unemployment among the medical profession, for instance, and to weaken the funeral as one of the main bonds of family life.

He recommends improving the quality of life by gradually weaning people away from unhealthy indoor forms of death, such as heart disease, and offering more facilities for dying traditional outward-looking deaths in the fresh air. To this end he urges the setting up of carefully landscaped mountains and waterless deserts in the main centres of population, and their stocking with carnivorous animals and poisonous reptiles.

The first two impressions of the report sell out before publication, and there is fierce competition for the paperback rights. The reviews are marvellous, and Howard gets a call from Bill Mishkin, of Bill Mishkin Productions.

'Howard Baker,' says Mishkin, 'I want to make this thing. It's as simple as that.'

Bill Mishkin has an office on the 54th floor of the RCA building. The hills outside the city are remote and blue behind his head as he leans back in his chair, shirt sleeves rolled up, collar and tie loosened. He is younger than Howard expected, with crisp curly hair, full smooth cheeks which are just about to smile, at his own jokes, but never quite do, and thick horn-rimmed spectacles through which his magnified eyes watch carefully to estimate audience reaction. The office is littered with scripts.

'Howard,' he says, 'I think this is far and away the subtlest, most exciting . . . *zaniest* . . . most realizable, wittiest, sexiest . . . *most lovable* White Paper that I have ever set eyes on.'

'Well . . .' says Howard politely.

'I love McKechnie. You know who McKechnie reminds me of? Raskolnikov. Only McKechnie's more subtle. I love the idea of lions and tigers in the middle of London. Like we're in Bond Street. Suddenly . . . rrrr rrrr! And there's a man-eating tiger bounding out of the Westbury Hotel! You have a very visual imagination, do you know that, Howard?'

'Well . . .' objects Howard modestly.

'No, you really do. And the mangrove swamps? There's this guy walking down Piccadilly, when suddenly – woomph! He's gone! "Help!" – schloomp, schloomp, schloomp – he's fallen into a mangrove swamp! Howard, you and I share the same sense of humour.'

'Well . . .' smiles Howard, tactfully.

'We're really going to have a ball together on this one. Because the thing is this, Howard. I want you to write the script.'

'Well . . .' agrees Howard cautiously.

'Because you're the only one who can do it, Howard. You understand these people. And it's practically a script already. Because I don't want to change *anything*. I want to realize exactly what you have envisioned.'

'Well . . .' says Howard gratefully.

'Did you by any chance get to see New Canaan, Connecticut, between 1 March and 14 April last year? No? Because that was mine. I made that. That would have given you some idea of the way I work. I also did one or two of those hijackings over Nevada – but that wouldn't have interested you. That was a different style of production altogether.

'I wish you'd seen New Canaan, Connecticut, 1 March to 14 April . . . Excuse me one minute. Stella, before Howard leaves, will you fix for him to fly to New Canaan for a few days last spring . . .?'

'Well . . .' considers Howard.

'Because I know you'll appreciate that. No violence. No unnecessary screwing. Just a lot of real people doing real things. A black family moves in – the neighbours bake them a cake. This young guy has an automobile accident – they take him to hospital – his wife breaks down and cries. That kind of thing. There are some really wacky scenes at the PTA meeting that you'd love. And the colour's just fantastic . . .'

'Well . . .' objects Howard.

'But this report of yours, Howard. Two years ago we couldn't have made this. The industry wasn't mature enough. But now the message is getting through. This is the kind of thing that people want to see. They're sick of big war spectaculars. They want a little idealism, a little love. The bankers realize they've bombed with the blockbusters. They're ready to back our judgment now, Howard – my judgment, your judgment.'

'Well . . .' accepts Howard graciously.

'This is a go project, Howard. Together we'll build Jerusalem in England's green and pleasant hills.'

———————————

'For the option,' Howard explained to Felicity, walking up and down the terrace, frowning seriously, with the setting sun flashing in a thousand windows of the city behind him,

'they're paying . . .   30.000,00

'They pay that anyway, what-ever happens.

'Then, if we go ahead with the script, they pay, for the treatment . . .   50.000,00
then for the first draft . . .   120.000,00
and for the second draft another   120.000,00
making in all, for the script . . .   290.000,00

'Then if we actually go ahead and build the New Jerusalem, they have to take up the full rights, which would amount to . . .   2.000.000.000,00.'

Felicity gazes at him, trying to take it in.   '2.000.000.000,00?'
She repeats.

'That's right,' says Howard casually . . .   '2.000.000.000,00.'

'I suppose it's all right,' says Felicity, 'if you say it quickly . . .   2.000.000.000,00 . . .'

'Oh,' says Howard . . .   '2.000.000.000,00
isn't all that much, as these

things go. After all . . .
when you think about it, is . . .
compared to the budget for the
whole production, which will   0,00
probably run out about . . .   2.000.000.000,00
100.000.000.000.000.000.000.000.000.000.000.000.000.00'

Bill Mishkin flies out to Rome. Bill Saltman, the director, flies in from Miami. He calls Howard as soon as he arrives – but Howard has flown out to the Bahamas, for a conference with Bill Mishkin, who is stopping over on his way to Caracas. But it turns out that Bill Mishkin has had to change his plans, and go to New York instead to get a haircut. So Howard flies out from the Bahamas just as Bill Saltman flies in.

Eventually Howard and Bill Saltman meet back home, two blocks away from the RCA building; but in Howard's case with a great sense of velocity from his journeyings.

Bill Saltman has rented a large apartment with no windows, Second Empire furnishings, and gunsmiths' production drawings of antique firearms arranged in tasteful cluster on the walls. He is a melancholy man, much older than Mishkin, with pouched drooping eyes that have seen civilizations fall and currencies collapse. He sits in a Second Empire armchair, a curling pipe in one side of his mouth, the other side opening and closing every few moments, like a fish breaking the surface, to let the smoke out, and listens expressionlessly while Howard explains his ideas for the script. Howard moves about the room, sitting on various chairs, gesturing.

'What I'm aiming at,' says Howard, 'is not some kind of thing where everybody is, you know, just sort of happy and sort of contented sort of thing all the time . . .'

The phone rings.

'Who did you say?' says Bill into the phone in a teasing voice, without taking the pipe out of his mouth, and looking blankly at Howard as he talks, as somewhere to rest his eyes. 'Biba? That's a very pretty name. Did you think that up yourself . . . No, I'm kidding, Biba . . . You know what, Biba? I don't know who you are and I can't understand what you're trying to tell me, but you have a very beautiful telephone voice, and I believe you have saved my life . . . No, I mean that, Biba, because I am sitting here totally alone, going slowly out of my mind. I have influenza and pains in my stomach. I'm dying, Biba. What is this terrible place . . .? Of course I'd love you to stop by, Biba : . . Bless you, Biba, bless you. An old man's blessing on your head.'

He puts the phone down.

'Go on,' he says to Howard.

'I'm sorry,' says Howard. 'I didn't know you were ill.'

Bill Saltman lifts his shoulders very slightly.

'It's the pills,' he says. 'The green and white pills I was prescribed in Athens. They don't go with the red pills I got in Miami. Go on.'

'Well,' says Howard, 'I think the thing we want to avoid at all costs – I mean, I really feel quite strongly about this – is setting up some kind of Utopia – some kind of oversimplified Arcadia which wouldn't stretch the imagination of the . . .'

The phone rings.

'Is this Jane?' says Bill Saltman. 'Oh, Gayle . . . You waited in the bar till midnight . . .? Honey, I'm sorry. I had to go to Tangier. Then I had to go to Miami. Then I had to go to Hawaii. Then I just felt so tired I thought

I'd have an early night. Well, come around six, Gayle –
I'm in a meeting for the next two three hours.'

He turns to Howard.

'So . . .?'

'So what I think we've got to do,' says Howard, 'is to
set up a society where everyone has enough sort of . . .
contentment . . . to be sort of contented, but not so
much that they can't see that all this sort of contentment is sort of blinding them to the possibility of becoming sort of *more* contented in a sort of kind of
deeper sort of . . .'

The doorbell rings. It's Biba. She is ridiculously young
and pretty, and flustered to find two of them.

'Excuse me, Howard,' says Bill. 'Could you look back
at five, say? I have a conference at six, but we could
get in one hour's work, at any rate. I think we should
make a serious effort to get progress on this thing.'

Howard can't help laughing to himself as he goes
down in the lift. What a world he's got himself into
now! Bill Saltman is a fantastic character – the kind of
quirky, tiresome man who actually gets extraordinary
things done; the kind of man who is so implausible as
the director of the New Jerusalem that you feel he
really might just possibly bring it off.

Howard strolls up Sixth Avenue in the afternoon
sunlight. How far he has come since the days in Harry
Fischer's office above the tobacconist's, with the cosy
office jokes and the lunchtime beers in the pub! Now he
is in a world where it's nothing to fly to the Bahamas
for a conference – and for a conference that's probably
not even going to *be* in the Bahamas; a world where
very high-class girls ring up uninvited and try to make
you feel at home.

His life has a vertiginous sense of development and
purpose.

'I've been thinking,' says Bill Saltman when Howard returns at five o'clock. He is smoking his curly pipe still, but is now wearing only a Turkish bathrobe and Persian slippers. There is no sign of Biba. A stuffiness lingers in the air – an overbreathed smell. He turns on the air-conditioner. The stale smell is replaced by a dank smell.

'I've been giving it a lot of thought,' he says slowly, chewing on the pipe, and smoothing the glossy black hair above the drooping face. 'I think I know where we've gone wrong. The thing is this, Howard. You've told me a lot about your ideas, and I've enjoyed sitting here listening to them. But tell me one thing, Howard. What's the story?'

'The story?' says Howard. He jumps up from the day-bed on which he has just sat down. 'Well . . .'

Bill Saltman holds up his hand.

'Just a moment, Howard. Would you excuse me for a moment? I have to take a shower. I'm awfully sticky.'

He disappears. Howard sinks back on to the day-bed. The *story*? He's never thought about it like that. A story . . . But this might be a good way to look at it – not as something static, but as a scenario, a sequence of events, a developing situation, something existing in a temporal dimension! He goes to the Chinese desk, and takes a sheet of paper out of the Mexican paper-rack.

Bill Saltman's head appears round the door, with fingers of wet hair hanging over his leathery brown forehead.

'So what's the story, Howard?' he demands.

'I'm just writing it.'

'Tell it me. I've left my reading glasses in Bangkok some place.'

'Well,' says Howard, jumping up, and beginning to walk up and down, 'it's the story of society, where everyone begins to get more and more aware of its real nature, and . . .'

'In two words, Howard. I'm standing here with water running off me.' —

'Well, people begin to make a structural analysis . . .'

'Hold it. I'll put some clothes on.'

When he comes back he is wearing a shirt and a pair of socks held up by suspenders.

'I'll tell you what a story is, Howard,' he says. 'A story is when something happens. A story is when someone's trying to do something, and someone's trying to stop him. So, wham, there's a fight on.'

'Yes, well . . .'

'A story is when this McTavish you have in the book – we'll have to change that name, by the way – they'll never believe it – they'll arrest you . . .'

'It's McKechnie.'

'That's worse. A story is when McTavish wants to build a better world for everyone – just like you have it in the book, I don't want to change anything – and the local hoods jump on him. Or his wife, even – she turns against him. How about that, Howard? His wife, his own wife! That could be good. "Oh God, Mary!" says McPherson. "Oh God, Mary!" – his voice is breaking with emotion – "Oh God, Mary, I don't want our kids to grow up in a world like this, with man an enemy to man, and cats crawling all over the books, in a cold-water walk-up behind the subway depot. I want a decent world where a man can stand on his own two feet, etcetera, etcetera, etcetera." '

'Yes, well . . .'

'Listen, Howard. And Mary says, "Don't make trouble, Lester! You'll lose your job! Haven't we always been happy together the way we are? You testify before the Commission tomorrow and I take the kids and go home to Mother in Milwaukee!" Now, that's a *story*, Howard!'

'But isn't this going to lead to violence, and, and . . .'

The doorbell rings.

'Let her in, Howard, while I put my pants on. I'll see you tomorrow, at twelve o'clock, and maybe we can get in an hour's work before lunch.'

So this is how it's going to be, thinks Howard, as he rides down in the lift again. An exhilarating struggle between the abstraction and intellectuality of his concept, and the strong vulgarity, the earthy vigour, of Bill Saltman's. This is the way things are created! How inturned and etiolated and over-educated Harry Fischer's design team seems now! It was only too appropriate that they were designing inert masses of rock with their noses in the air, and snow on them.

Gayle was pretty, too.

'But Bill Mishkin,' shouts Howard, 'said specifically that it doesn't have to be all sex and violence.'

Shouting is one of the useful skills he is learning. This is several days later.

'Bill Mishkin,' says Bill Saltman, 'is a simple Russian boy from way out in the sticks who went through law school and inherited a couple of million from his uncle in the garment trade and couldn't add two and two together and get more than four.'

'Bill Mishkin's just made New Canaan, Connecticut, 1 March to 14 April, without so much as a single shooting, beating, or naked buttock from one end to the other! Just whites being nice to blacks, and parents smoking a little sympathetic pot with their kids!'

'Right! So who's ever seen it? Who's ever heard of it? New Canaan, Connecticut, 1 March to 14 April, has just sunk like a stone, disappeared without trace!'

'Look, I'm not arguing about the rapes. I see we need those. I admit that. And the burning alive bits, and the flagellation, and the cannibalism. All I'm saying is that we'll overdo it if we have the . . .'

The phone rings.

'Hello?' says Bill. 'Oh no, not again! But this is the third time she's escaped! What are the guards *for* . . .?'

He put his hand over the mouthpiece.

'It's family business,' he says to Howard. 'Could you come back at about ten o'clock tonight . . .?'

'Oh God, it's going to be a terrible place!' cries Howard to his fellow-guests around the Chases' dinner table, holding his head and rocking it from side to side in humorous despair.

'You know Howard's writing the scenario for the New Jerusalem, don't you?' Prue reminds them all.

'The New Jerusalem!' cries Howard. 'More like the New Disneyland, by the time we've finished! I can't tell you the dreck we're going to have in it. I shall never be able to look anyone in the eye again. Would you believe *gladiator shows*? And *public hangings*?'

They all laugh – but with a tinge of envy and respect.

'It sounds like a real Howard Baker story,' says Barratt Kessel. But he's impressed, Howard can tell, by the casual use of expressions like 'dreck' and 'would you believe?'

'If it ever gets made,' says Howard. 'Because I don't think it's ever going to get off the ground. You wouldn't believe the wheeling and dealing that's going on.'

'Tell us anyway,' says Charles Aught.

'Well,' says Howard, 'it turns out that Mishkin doesn't actually have any money himself. He's simply trying to put a package together to sell to one of the big corporations – Ehyeh-Asher-Ehyeh or Zebaot International. To do that, of course, he has to have some bankable names to star in it. Like Joan of Arc and St Francis of Assissi. Don't laugh – I'm serious. But of course Joan's tied up in the Hundred Years' War, and Frank's got involved in some great animal epic. And while we're waiting for *them*, Bill Saltman's gone off to direct the establishment of white slavery in South America. Still, I'm learning the general principles of the business. In five words: Grab the money and run.'

They all avoid his eye, they are so awed. He is developing morally, this is the point. He is learning to enjoy a new range of sour and bitter flavours, of gamey meat and dungy cheese, to set off the wholesome bread of his daily life. For the fabric of his life has not changed at all. He obstinately continues to love his wife and children, to be moved to tears by music, and to be disturbed by the sun breaking between banks of cloud, low in the sky over flat muddy fields on a winter's afternoon.

And there could scarcely be anything more difficult and fine-textured than the affair he is having with a woman called Rose. She is dark and serious. She has creases at the corners of her eyes, and when she lowers her head to avoid Howard's serious gaze she has a fold of flesh under her jaw.

She lives in a comfortable shabby house covered in crumbling stucco, with an overgrown garden full of great elms and sycamores, which fill the house with a soft green light. There are three cats. She plays the piano a lot. The whole house has a rather appalling familiarity about it.

She can't see Howard often, because of her husband, whom she loves, and her children. Even when they do meet, on flat overcast weekday afternoons at her house, it's often hopeless. She moves restlessly back and forth between living-room and kitchen, feeding the cats, picking up children's boots, looking for a letter she was writing. He trails after her, making dramatic declarations of a sort he never has the occasion to make to Felicity.

'I *love* you!' he cries. 'Can't you understand that? I want you! I need you! But you don't love me at all! Do you?'

'Of course I do,' she says, making a little kissing sound. 'I must just finish this letter. It's my cousin.'

That's the sort of woman she is – the sort of woman who has cousins. She also has an aunt who as a girl in Oxford knew several famous philosophers.

It's extremely improbable that someone who is working with people like Bill Mishkin and Bill Saltman should be having an affair with someone like Rose. He tries to explain this to her. He tries to convey to her the vital importance that their complex relationship has to him as a counterpoint to his work on the New Jerusalem. She sits curled up in the corner of the sofa with her feet tucked under her and her half-written letter to her cousin waiting in her lap. Long wisps of dark hair fall across her face. She pushes them away, gazing at Howard sombrely.

'My work,' he says, 'depends upon my having some kind of . . . *depth*. Some kind of moral complexity and ambiguity. Our whole involvement in the world is devious. It has to be devious. We're working in a complex and difficult medium. That's why I need you.'

She yawns.

'Oh God,' says Howard.

'Sorry,' says Rose. 'I was thinking about my cousin,

114

not about you.'

She writes her letter. The cover on the sofa is rumpled. Next to Rose there is a muddle of books and mending, and a flute, and one of the cats. The pattern on the carpet is worn threadbare. An old clock ticks slowly. On the mantelpiece letters and invitations and bills are stuffed behind little Staffordshire pots.

He loves the opacity of her life, its completeness without him. But it's exactly that completeness which makes him suffer so. Suffering in love is one of the new bitter flavours he has learnt to appreciate. How he suffers! He suffers so much he wants to weep.

So, hell, he weeps.

Why not? After all, nothing is a joke here, as it is at home with Felicity. Every moment he grows deeper.

He goes out to the kitchen to hide his tears.

'Put some coffee on,' calls Rose.

The enamel coffee-pot is chipped. There is an old coffee-grinder on the wall with a camellia lacquered on it, and a loose, rusty handle.

Slowly the water comes to the boil. The clock ticks. How sad life is! How deep and sad!

When Howard comes tragically back with the coffee, Rose is no longer alone. There is a man sitting in the rocking-chair opposite her, hunched over a book. A bespectacled man with stand-up hair, who has taken his shoes off and hung his feet over the arm of the chair. There is a hole in his right sock.

'Phil!' cries Howard, in astonishment.

Phil looks up briefly.

'Black for me, please,' he says.

Howard struggles not to feel appalled. But, really, what's Rose going to make of *this*? She'll think he invited Phil! Told him to look in any time – just to walk in, sit down, take his shoes off, and make himself at home! She'll think he's presuming upon their relationship. As if the situation weren't difficult enough anyway!

'I'm sorry,' he says to Rose. 'I didn't know Phil was coming.'

'I must just finish this letter,' says Rose.

Howard pours the coffee, trying to feel that the whole situation is normal.

'But what I don't understand,' he says to Phil, smiling conversationally, 'is what you're *doing* here.'

'Reading Jeremiah,' says Phil.

'It's a waste of time name-dropping with me,' says Howard easily, as he fetches another coffee mug from the dresser. 'I don't know who you're talking about. Jeremiah who?'

Phil turns back the pages of his book, frowning.

'That's funny,' he murmurs. 'It doesn't say.'

'Oh, *Jeremiah*!' says Howard. He laughs, entirely at his ease, and puts seven lumps of sugar into his coffee.

'I'm always making a Phil of myself with fool,' he explains to Rose. He fishes the seven lumps of sugar out of his coffee. Then he puts two of them back.

Rose remains bent over her letter, Phil over Jeremiah. What an odd situation! Howard gets up and walks about the room with his coffee, smiling, and taking care not to fall over the furniture. Actually he is rather pleased that Rose should see he has friends as eccentrically impressive as Phil, and that Phil should see he is having an affair with someone as solid and opaque as Rose, whose aunt as a girl in Oxford knew several famous philosophers.

But why are they too shy to look at each other?

He leans back against the mantelpiece with his coffee,

mastering the situation, a man of the world entertaining his oldest friend in his mistress's house.

'I think we must get that husband of yours to lop a few branches off outside the window before you go blind,' he says to Rose, to demonstrate the terms he is on with her. To Phil he says: 'I saw quite a number of the men you're doing when I was in London. I got the impression you had problems. A lot of the models I saw had snags you hadn't really got ironed out. I thought.'

Which tells Rose the kind of terms he is on with Phil.

'Yes,' says Phil, without looking up, 'I read your report.'

'I tried to play it down in the report.'

'Oh. Thanks.'

'I couldn't suppress it entirely, of course.'

'No.'

'I mean, we have problems, too, with the New Jerusalem.'

'Yes.'

All the same, there is something irritating about the way Phil sits there taking everything so much for granted – his presence in the house, Howard's discretion in the report, even the coffee.

'Well,' says Howard pointedly, looking at his watch, 'we must talk about it some time.'

'Talk about it now, if you like,' says Phil.

'I mean,' says Howard quite bluntly, 'it's probably time to go, isn't it?'

'Not at all,' says Phil. 'Stay as long as you like. Have an apple. Have two apples. Stay to dinner.'

Howard stares at him, then at Rose. His perspective of them changes as he stares. It's like one of those cube patterns which pops inside out, from convex to concave, in front of your eyes.

'I see,' he says heavily. 'I see. I suppose I've been

making a fool of myself. I should have guessed that something like this was going on. Well, well, well. I think I'm entitled to feel rather bitter.'

He feels justifiably bitter for some minutes.

The door opens and a boy enters. He has spectacles and stand-up hair, and is trailing a satchel on the floor behind him. 'Mum,' he says to Rose, 'I had a fight with James Dunn today, and guess who won? Is it teatime yet?

'Dad,' he says to Phil, 'if one side had hydrogen bombs and the other side didn't, but they had about say a trillion ordinary bombs, well, which side would win?'

'Not yet,' says Rose.

'I don't know,' says Phil.

'Can I watch television?' says the boy.

He goes out, leaving his satchel on the floor. Howard gazes after him, flabbergasted.

'You mean,' says Howard, 'you're *married?*'

'Didn't you get an invitation?' asks Phil. 'Deckle-edged? With silver bells on the front? About eleven years ago? Don't say we forgot to send you one.'

'Me!' cries Howard, walking about the upper roof garden of his converted dungeon. 'Having an affair with the wife of my oldest friend!'

Felicity, lying back with her eyes closed in the late afternoon sun, smiles.

'I always thought Rose was deeper than you gave her credit for,' she says.

'I *knew* I knew the house! I knew I knew the telephone number!'

'You are a fool,' says Felicity tenderly.

'But that it should happen to *me*! This is the kind of situation other people get into!'

'You always underestimate yourself so,' says Felicity. 'If other people can get themselves into these situations, so can you.'

He sits down. His elbows rest on his knees. He gazes at the ground.

'You don't understand,' he groans. 'I've shouted at her. I've burst into tears. Shouted and wept at someone else's wife!'

She puts her hand on his.

'I knew I wasn't the only person in the world you'd got the courage to shout at,' she says.

Howard sighs.

'But imagine Phil came round here and shouted at *you*,' he says.

She laughs.

'That's the difference between you,' she says. 'He wouldn't. He *couldn't*.'

Howard puts his face in his hands.

'Don't be silly,' says Felicity. 'This is a completely new departure for you. You can't go on forever just playing with the children and telling self-deprecating stories about yourself at the Chases' dinner-parties. Just at the moment other men are beginning to wonder if they've come to the end of themselves, and if this is all that life has to offer, you discover a complete new range of abilities in yourself. You find you can betray your friends, and suffer, and inflict suffering on others. You've unearthed a completely new range of possibilities in your character.'

'That may be true,' says Howard, looking away with tragic restraint. 'But there's much more to it than that. What I feel goes much deeper than that. You don't understand.'

'You mean,' says Felicity, 'it makes you think that this whole society is morally ambiguous. You see that we're all implicated in deception and betrayal. It's a real crisis in your life.'

He says nothing.

'I understand you very well, you see,' she says.

'Then why do you let the children leave their bicycles in the cloister?' he shouts. 'I've told you about it a thousand times.'

He turns his back upon the life he has led in this society. Its moral confusion disgusts him.

He resigns from the New Jerusalem. They sell up. They take the children out of school. They will live simply in the country.

The night before they move Howard sits on the terrace looking down upon the city for the last time. The great landscape of lights glitters and shimmers in the warm evening air. The diamond rivers of traffic flow inexhaustibly on. It is no less beautiful to him than on that first night. But now its beauty seems lost and sinister. He is looking at a bewitched forest of crystal trees and jewelled flowers, rooted in the black soil, breathing black air.

Somewhere down there his friends are going about their lives, laughing in the blackness. That car there, in the stream of lights flowing along the Parkway – that might be the Waylands. Michael will be driving. 'Just tell me who's likely to be there this evening,' he's saying. 'Just run through their names. Then I'll be all right.'

'I think Prue said Laurence and Shirley Esplin will be there,' Myra is saying. 'Then probably either Charles Aught or Bill Goody, and perhaps Jack and Miriam . . .'

(But maybe *those* are the Bernsteins now, in the car

there, crossing over the top of the Parkway on the Uptown Expressway, going not to the Chases' at all, but to the Kessels' . . .)

'. . . And of course,' adds Myra, as she looks up at the lights on the hills where the Bakers live, 'Howard and Felicity.'

'I wonder,' Miriam Bernstein is saying to Jack, craning her head to look up at those same lights, 'if Howard and Felicity will be there . . .'

Howard's heart goes out to them – to Michael and Myra, to Jack and Miriam, to Roy and Prue – to all of them down there in the glittering darkness. From his great height in the hills he loves them and sorrows for them. For what he understands, and what they apparently do not, or will not, is that the whole lovely complex crystal machine in which they live is built upon suffering and death.

Phil was right: there is no metropolis without provinces, no administrators without administered, no doctors without disease. The flaws which they are building into the system (which even Phil is building into the system) – the endemic morbidity – are not incidental but essential. They are the weakness which can be exploited to keep men at work producing the goods which this society needs, and to keep them in subjection.

And they are all implicated. They are all working the system. Even if his New Jerusalem were ever built it would be executed and administered by the people in this city. It would be populated by Phil's creations – patched up and improved a bit, but still the products of this same society.

And he is the only one who can see this! He himself, standing exactly here in the darkness above the city, with the night breeze ruffling his hair. Old Howard Baker, everyone's friend, the slightly comic figure with the earnest expression on his face leading the way down the street for the rest of his body, the man who innocently believes whatever he is told, and gets everything slightly wrong.

A small noise behind him makes him turn round. Felicity is standing in the doorway of the living-room.

'What is it?' he asks.

'I was just looking at you against the lights of the city,' she says. 'You're very slightly phosphorescent.'

He puts his arm round her and goes back indoors. They take another load of accumulated junk down to the dustbins. One of the biggest items is the complete working model of their life which he bought the children for Christmas all those years ago. As he buckles it and breaks it to get it in the bin, a strange sweet sadness rises to his throat.

They are living in a ramshackle old farmhouse in the woods. Once the land round it was worked, but no one these days would break his back over soil so rocky and barren. The primaeval forest has closed in again all around.

'The relief!' cries Howard, as he goes about in an old pair of jeans, mending the roof and painting the window-frames. 'The sense of liberation when you really give everything up, and own nothing. I realize now that somewhere inside myself this is what I was always longing for.'

They do in fact own almost literally nothing, except the house, and a few acres of the surrounding woodland to serve as a no-man's land between them and the world. They have a few sheep, to keep down the poison ivy, a few pigs to breed, and a dusty station wagon to take them to market.

The children run wild, in shirts and jeans.

For an hour or two each day, no more, Howard and Felicity take it in turns to teach them. They do a little arithmetic, a little Greek and Italian, a little harmony and counterpoint. They read Dante and Tacitus and St Augustine together, with the Authorized Version and Gibbon to develop the style. Nothing else.

The inside of the house is almost bare of furniture. Just plain white walls and stripped floors, and the simplest of old tables and chairs. Their voices ring out cheerfully from the uncluttered surfaces.

They set aside a room for Howard to work in, when he's not labouring outside with an axe or a scythe. A table. A chair. A typewriter. He is putting a few thoughts down on paper.

Felicity bakes the bread, singing.

Once or twice a week Howard climbs into the station wagon and drives over to the little market town fifteen miles away. Buys paraffin for the lamps, flour, nails, bubblegum for the children. Picks up the mail and the newspapers. Drops into the bank.

Bees fly in through the windows on hot afternoons, zigzag across the house, and disappear through the open front door. The scent of cow-parsley in the lane is overwhelming.

The children find an injured fox cub, and rear it.

It rains. A mist of rain hangs in the tops of the trees. Howard lights a fire of the pine logs he has cut, and they sit in front of it with tumblers of neat Irish whiskey. Howard has *Paradise Lost* open on his knee, Felicity the *Faerie Queen*. The children are reading old *Chums* annuals.

'What did we need a television set for?' demands Howard wonderingly. 'Do you remember the television, children?'

The children laugh.

'There's only one good thing about that society,' says

Howard, 'and that's the opportunity it offers you to reject it.'

In this little world of sheep, pigs, bread-oven, and books, closely bounded on all sides by the surrounding woods, the whole tenor of his thinking begins to alter. He sees that the grandiose, monumental scale on which the universe is being planned is wrong in itself, even apart from the physical risks it will entail.

What's the *purpose* of mountains ten and twenty thousand feet high? Of oceans three miles deep and a thousand miles across? Of miraculously complicated organisms so small that they can be seen only by a privileged élite, through microscopes costing several thousand pounds? Of vistas of stars set at distances too great for the human mind to comprehend? Of the vertiginous emptiness between and beyond the stars?

Of the universe of ooos and ooo.ooos and ooo.ooo.ooos – a universe of zeros?

It seems to him, as he sits in his little white room, on a plain elm chair, at a plain oak table, with a view of green leaves outside the plain square window, and a plain old-fashioned black portable typewriter waiting beneath his fingers, that the purpose of all this massive display of hardware is clear : it is to overawe the minds of men and to symbolize their subjugation.

There must be a revolution. There is no other way.

The people must seize power and create their own universe. The millennium cannot be imposed on them from above.

The universe which men will create for themselves, after they have thrown off the tyranny of Phil Schaffer, Roy Chase, himself, and the rest of them, will be a very different sort of place. He envisages it in a kind of ecstasy – a world made by man, to man's scale, for man to live in.

A world of gently undulating landscapes, made of some shock-absorbent material like foam rubber, on which it would be impossible to injure yourself.

Of oceans fresh enough to drink, too shallow to drown in, and narrow enough for children to wade across, shrimping net in hand, from Southampton to New York.

Of ice warm enough to warm the hands on.

Of air too thick for aircraft to fall out of.

Of bacteria the size of hamsters, living peaceably in imaginatively landscaped enclosures at the zoo.

A world set in a universe whose furthest reaches could be explored by any rambler with a pair of nailed boots, a packet of sandwiches, and a one-inch map.

And men must be free to create themselves. This is the keystone of his conception.

There will be no more breakable bones or shoddy arteries. No more below-average intellects. No more excuses for death.

Each man will decide for himself how many arms and legs he wants, and whether he wants white skin or black skin, or whether he'd prefer to be covered in furnishing fabric or mink.

A people's world, and a people's people.

It's Miriam Bernstein who tracks them down.

'Don't hesitate to offer me a large drink!' she squeaks, as she climbs out of her car one sultry afternoon, and they all emerge from the house, astonished, Howard and the boys stripped to the waist. 'I had to phone fourteen different estate agents before I found the one you'd dealt with . . . My God, but you're so brown and sinewy!'

It's irritating to see her there, all nervy and squeaky,

in her clothes for motoring out to the country in; but oddly touching and pleasing that she should have come.

'Why didn't you *tell* anyone you were leaving? Well, obviously, because you wanted to get away from us all . . . But when you never answered the phone, and Prue went round to your house, and found *carriage lamps* outside the front door, and some terrible people with *poodles* inside, it was a terrible shock. The poodle people said you'd thrown everything up and gone off to live in a shack in the country . . . I say, what a *super* house – I'm only just taking it in . . . And I thought what a smashing idea for a television programme! Someone terribly successful and important and super like you turning your back on it all. What's wrong with our society? kind of thing . . . Oh, I suppose you haven't heard: I've gone into television, now all the children are at school. Bill Goody knew someone who knew someone. I think in the office they think I'm rather an idiot. So if I could go back and say, "Hurrah! I've found Howard Baker! I've persuaded him to let us film an exclusive interview with him in his secret retreat!" it would be a colossal boost for me. You will say yes, won't you, Howard? For me? If I flutter my eyelashes at you, and promise to bake you one of my apple crumbles?'

Howard smiles, and frowns, and thinks about it seriously as they all have tea in the orchard, and Miriam, in her dark glasses and clothes for motoring out to the country in, smokes furiously to keep away the insects, and chatters on about what happened when they went to dinner with the Chases the previous week, and Michael Wayland forgot Prue's name!

How shallow, how futile, how desperate that world sounds now, on the scythed grass, beneath the trees where the fruit they will conserve for the winter is ripening.

All the same, he can scarcely refuse to help Miriam in

her career, it seems to him, just because he himself has turned his back on that world and its career-making.

Besides, it will be an opportunity to expound the ideas he has been developing.

'And visually,' says Miriam, 'with all these trees and sheep and things, and the children running about, it should be an absolute *riot*.'

_____

'I warn you – I'm not going to pull any punches,' Howard tells Miriam when she comes back the following week with the film crew. 'It's going to be straight revolutionary stuff.'

'Super,' says Miriam. 'The wilder the better, as far as we're concerned.'

A dozen men move back and forth, putting up lights in the living-room, shifting all the furniture round, and accepting trays of tea from Felicity in the kitchen.

'I'm not going to turn myself into a performing monkey,' warns Howard. 'I'm not going to do anything I don't genuinely do in my everyday life here.'

'Of course not,' says Miriam. 'That's the whole point of the programme.'

They sit him in the rocking-chair in front of the hearth, to rock himself back and forth as he muses out loud about the enslavement of man by natural technology.

'I don't want to fuss,' he says, 'but the rocking-chair is usually over by the wall, not in front of the hearth.'

'Don't worry,' says the director. 'It's just that we have to see the hearth if we're to know you're in an old farmhouse. If we shoot you against a blank wall you might be in the middle of the city, or in the studio, or anywhere. That's why I've moved the bookcase behind your head. If we can't see *The Decline and Fall of the Roman Empire* in the shot it doesn't *exist.*'

'I see,' says Howard reasonably.

Later they go outside, and the camera tracks in front of him as he walks about the property, prodding a pig here and shearing a sheep there, explaining how, left to themselves, people logically cannot fail to humanize the universe.

All the while the cameraman is walking backwards the assistant cameraman walks behind him, holding him by the waist and steering him round children's bicycles and feed-troughs.

When Howard leans on a gate, talking about the rottenness of the society he has rejected, his children are in frame as well, rather small in the background, playing tag next to his left ear.

He is standing on a box to bring his head into line with them.

———

The children are allowed to sit up and watch the programme when it finally goes out (Howard has bought a small portable television set for the occasion). As soon as it's over the phone rings (they've had a phone put in so that they can get bread and groceries delivered, and feel less cut off from doctors and fire services).

It's Prue.

'Prue!' exclaims Howard, very pleased to hear the familiar impossible voice at such a moment, when he is feeling so raw and exposed from watching himself, and so uncertain whether he is a great man or a great fool.

'Miriam and Jack are here,' says Prue, 'and the Way-lands, and the Kessels, and Luci Hayter, and we all thought you were *lovely*.'

A grateful warmth spreads out through Howard's head from his telephone ear.

'Did you really think it was all right, Prue? Only it's so difficult judging what kind of impression one's making, out here on one's own.'

'You were *perfect*. We've all been congratulating Miriam. The real vintage Howard. We've all missed you dreadfully. We've all talked about nothing else, ever since you went. It's cast a terrible gloom over everything.'

He realizes as she says it how much he's been missing *her* and all the rest of them. He makes haste to tell her so.

'Oh, nonsense,' she cries. 'You're having a marvellous time out there. You've just been telling us all what a relief it was to get out of the city.'

Good heavens, she doesn't think . . .!

'Prue!' he says anxiously. 'I hope you didn't think I was getting at you and Roy. I mean with all that stuff about little coteries, and cosy dinner-parties, and so on . . .'

'*Dear* Howard – please don't worry about it. We were all really rather impressed. We all felt that you'd managed to express some of the muddled worries we'd had about things ourselves.'

Howard walks back to the living-room smiling to himself. How pleasantly embarrassing to think of them all, sitting round the set at the Chases', making affectionately malicious remarks about his appearance and mannerisms!

But he has time to walk up and down the room only five times, telling Felicity what Prue said, before the phone rings again.

This time it's Bill Goody.

'I've just got your number from Prue,' he says. 'I thought I'd ring and congratulate you on managing at last to see what some of us have been going on about for all these years.'

This is an extraordinary compliment, coming from Bill, who is systematically sceptical and rude to almost everyone.

The next time the phone rings it's Charles Aught. Also in agreement. *Charles Aught!*

'But Charles,' says Howard, bewildered. 'I thought you were completely cynical about the whole thing? Don't you remember that lunch we had, where I lost my temper? That was what set me thinking in the first place.'

'Howard love, all I get the tiniest bit cynical about is the way everyone closes his eyes to the truth. I was only teasing you because I thought you were just like the rest of them. I obviously got you wrong.'

'No, at that time you were right — I *had* got my eyes closed. I clearly got *you* wrong.'

'Oh, I've always been a bit of a subversive. I don't know whether you saw any of the rather naughty stuff I put old Percy Bysshe up to?'

So he is not alone in his views, after all. Here and there in that hard, shining city there are individuals who think the same way as he does. Moles burrowing away underground, out of sight of each other, but with a common purpose. A group apart, the links between them welded by the sheer weight of society pressing down upon them.

He walks up and down for a while outside, unable to settle to the prospect of going to bed. The house gleams in the moonlight; the roses he has planted, now flooding the night with perfume, appear jet black and pure white.

Perhaps, in their reorganized solar system, they will keep the moon.

Even Phil phones.

'The bit I liked best,' says Phil, 'was when you prodded the pig and told it about the unfairness of micro-organisms. I thought you had the best of that particular discussion.'

Which, thinks Howard, may not sound much like a compliment – but which sounds considerably more like a compliment than anything else Phil has ever said.

He is the voice of his circle, his generation. This is how he is forced to see himself now.

And his circle, his generation, have a leading role to play in the establishment of a popular universe. The universe must be made by the people. But the people cannot make the universe themselves, without the aid of skilled and dedicated designers like Phil Schaffer and administrators like Bill Goody. He understands that now. They won't know what sort of universe to want. Without expert encouragement by people who know how to handle public relations, like Charles Aught, they may not even know they want *anything*.

It's not that he wishes to set himself up as a leader. But being outside the pressures of life in the city he has time to think, and to formulate his thoughts on all the issues of the day in the form of letters to the editors of the more influential newspapers. Whether it's the effect of the country air, or of all that Gibbon and Johnson, he doesn't know, but his prose style is transformed. After a few false starts a whole vocabulary and syntax that he never knew he knew begins to well up from his old-fashioned black portable. 'Sir . . . growing concern . . . today more than ever . . . the need for a sense of urgency . . . there are many of us who feel . . . protest in the strongest possible terms . . . how long must we wait before . . .? which I for one believe . . . make our voices heard . . .'

The effect is astonishing. It turns out that it is not just his own set and his own age-group that he speaks for. Letters pour into the correspondence columns from all over – some of them from people who sound several years older than himself, and some of them from the most exclusive neighbourhoods, well beyond the pockets of any of his friends.

'Sir,' they say, 'thank God there is someone . . . restored my faith in human nature . . . performed a signal service . . . struck a blow for common sense and ordinary human decency . . . exposed the hypocrisy of those who for our sins are set in authority over us . . . expressed what the vast majority of people feel . . . spoken up for the minority whose views are never taken into account . . .'

The reactionaries hit blindly back, 'Sir,' they retort, 'it was with some amusement that I read the views . . . with astonishment . . . with disgust . . . self-appointed guardians of the public conscience . . . fashionable cant . . . appear to have forgotten those who, in two world wars . . .' But they succeed only in making themselves look ridiculous.

People begin to write to him direct, seeking his collaboration in joint letters. To his surprise he finds himself basically in agreement on a wide range of questions which he has never really thought about before. He finds himself calling upon the Government to use its powers to stop or sink Christopher Columbus's expedition before it reaches America, and sets off a chain of events disastrous to the ecology of two continents. He deplores the Government's opening of the Red Sea to the Children of Israel, as old-fashioned interventionism of the most blatant sort. Utterly condemns the destruction of Sodom and Gomorrah. Welcomes, with some reservations, the introduction of the Black Death as a vital measure of population control.

He often comes down to the evening meal drained and exhausted after a day of writing his name at the bottom of letters like these. It's not easy, as he explains to Felicity, to sign your support for the Black Death, when you have previously expressed your opposition to nephritis, nephrosis, and heart disease. But the important thing is to maintain solidarity, to find common ground between all the different dissenting groups.

Because the people who think as he does are no longer a beleaguered minority. Invisibly, beneath its glass and steel surface, the whole city is changing. Behind the smiling faces a complete new philosophy of life is being thought out.

A transformed society is being born within the fabric of the old.

The city has become like one of the supersaturated solutions which Howard remembers making in the chemistry laboratory at school. When the last crystal is dropped in, the whole solution will suddenly crystallize out around it. At one stroke the water will cease to contain the salt, and the salt will contain the water.

––––––––––

The Chases drive out to spend the weekend with them. Then the Bernsteins, and the Waylands, and Charles Aught.

'What a *heavenly* place!' they each cry in turn, as they climb out of their cars, white-faced from the city and crumpled from the journey, and stroll with Howard across the lawns to the house in the evening sunshine.

'We're getting it right slowly,' shrugs Howard. 'You should have seen it when we first arrived. The trees and undergrowth came almost up to the house. The only furniture we had was a few tables and chairs.'

It's a great pleasure seeing their friends again like this after so along. They eat, drink wine, play croquet, and talk. Talk for hours, strolling along the gravel walks in the sleepy heat of the afternoon, or sitting round the great fireplace at night. Talk seriously and deeply – about themselves, about their regard and affection for each other, about the strangeness of life.

They and their guests never get on each other's nerves, because they have self-contained accommodation in what used to be the barns and outhouses. Howard converted them with his own hands, as he did everything else on the property.

The children never bother them. The Baker children take all the others off to the paddock, and teach them to ride.

These weekend visits are such a success that Howard and Felicity begin to expand them into full-scale house-parties – the Chases, the Waylands, and Luci Hayter, all at once; the Bernsteins, the Goodys, the Chyldes, and Charles Aught; the Kessels, the Keats, the Schaffers, the Chases, and Francis Fairlie. There are mixed doubles all afternoon, and Scrabble and acting games and trying on trunk-loads of period clothes all evening.

'It's just like Cliveden or Garsington!' cries Prue.

'It's just like the Chases',' replies Howard smoothly.

It is, too. They have absorbed the Chases' role.

'We are a *set*, aren't we?' says Miriam Bernstein. 'We're a sort of movement. We have our own style and ideas and ways of looking at things.'

But it's really not just a closed coterie. Their friends bring *their* friends down for the weekend. People begin to arrive uninvited, so that Howard and Felicity find themselves keeping more or less open house. The process snowballs, until suddenly *everything* is happening around their swimming-pool. Agents make deals with producers. Politicians gang up on each other. Love affairs start. People Howard has never heard of pick quarrels and pass out.

One or two ladies from the village come up and help out on these occasions, so that the Spanish couple don't have to do all the work. They love every minute of it, too, bless their hearts – particularly the scandals, and Howard strolls benignly among the guests, squeezing an elbow here, kissing a cheek there, making sure that everyone's got everything he wants.

'On second thoughts,' says Prue, 'I don't mean Garsington. I mean West Egg.'

'West Egg . . . ?' queries Howard.

'Where Gatsby lived.'

Howard smiles. The solution is thickening around him, moment by moment. Soon the last crystal will be dropped in, and transform everything.

It's Prue herself who finds the crystal.

One Saturday evening she takes Howard by the arm and leads him away from the crowd round the pool and the bar, out of everyone's earshot.

'Howard,' she says, in a special offhand voice, 'Freddie's here.'

'Oh good,' says Howard, smiling and nodding, unable to remember who Freddie is. 'I'm glad he could make it.'

'We called at the Barclays on the way down, and he was staying there for the weekend. He said he'd always wanted to meet you, so we brought them all over.'

'I look forward to meeting him,' says Howard urbanely. With all this practice he has become an unshakably well-mannered host.

Prue steers him discreetly towards the house. He discreetly allows himself to be steered.

'He's absolutely *charming*,' she says. 'But he hates crowds – I think he's really rather shy. So he's retired into the kitchen, of all places, and we're having to feed him people to meet one by one, like birds bringing back food for their young.'

As soon as Howard sees him he realizes why Prue is so specially calm and matter-of-fact. It's Freddie Vigars! The Honourable A. P. J. Vigars, who was at Cambridge two years ahead of Howard; the retiring figure in Trinity of whom all the great men of Howard's generation were in awe. They were in awe of him because you would never have guessed from meeting him how immensely wealthy he was, and because you would never have guessed from knowing how immensely wealthy he was how immensely clever he was as well, and because he was called Freddie when his initials were A. P. J. You'd catch a glimpse of this tall, stooped figure crossing Trinity Great Court, with one shoulder held slightly higher than the other, and you'd know you were watching one of the world's great fortunes walking about, plus, on the same two lanky legs, behind the same untidily dangling forelock, one of the world's great instruments of serious scholarship.

He is sitting on the corner of the big table in the kitchen, nodding his head and nibbling a dry biscuit, as Shirley Esplin, the flautist, explains about her work to him. She is talking rather too volubly, waving her hand. 'Yur,' he nods, 'yur . . . yur . . .' His head is cocked slightly to one side, as if to reduce his height to Shirley Esplin's level, and a slight sympathetic smile goes up one side of his face. His benevolent brown eyes are looking at the floor to Shirley's left, about five feet beyond her, and he appears to be thinking not about the flute as a career, but about the problems and opportunities of kitchen floor tiling.

He has scarcely changed at all. If anything, he looks slightly younger than Howard now. He is wearing a rather old-fashioned three-piece suit, made of a material that's far too thick for comfort, with turn-ups on the trousers. It's cut rather oddly about the shoulders, so that the collar of his shirt sticks out above it. The knot of his tie has slipped and worked round sideways, revealing a brass collar-stud. One scuffed heavy shoe is braced against the floor, the other dangles in space, with the turn-up riding high above it to reveal a thick grey sock crumpled around the ankle.

But the ladies from the village who are helping out look curiously at him, and call him sir when they rescue the spoons he is sitting on.

'Freddie,' says Prue, 'this is Howard Baker.'

'We did meet once, as a matter of fact,' says Howard, as they shake hands. 'It was in Trinity. I was walking across Great Court with Nick Simpkin. You invited him in for a glass of sherry to ask him if you could borrow his bicycle, and I came too.'

'Oh, really?' says Freddie, bending his lips upwards on one side of his face into a suggestion of general benevolence, but moving them only sparingly for the purpose of articulation. 'I'm sorry. I didn't . . .'

'Howard Baker,' repeats Prue.

'There's no reason why you should remember it,' says Howard. 'I just happened to be with Nick Simpkin. I don't suppose you remember *him*, for that matter . . .'

But the generalized smile on Freddie's face has dissolved. The head has moved upright on its mountings, and the eyebrows have risen half-an-inch.

'Howard Baker?' he says. 'Do forgive me. Crashing in like this. Wanted to meet you for years. Admired all your things. Enormous pleasure.'

Howard is too astonished to say anything. That Freddie Vigars should have heard of him! That Freddie Vigars should be sitting in front of him, shyly brushing the forelock out of his eyes in apparent awe! He brushes the forelock out of his own eyes, no less awed.

'Oh!' he says. 'That's extremely . . .'

'Absolutely *terrific.'*

'Well, that is immensely . . .'

'Really *tremendous.'*

'That is terrifically . . .'

'No, no. Enormously . . .'

'Well, that is immensely . . .'

Shirley Esplin and Prue, seeing that this is a private conversation, discreetly withdraw.

'Terrific surprise when you meet someone face to face,' says Freddie. 'I thought you'd look entirely different.'

'No . . . no . . .' says Howard. 'I look pretty much like this.'

'Terrible to think I once had you sipping sherry in my rooms and never realized it. Entertaining angels unawares.'

He laughs – surprisingly loudly, looking straight into Howard's eyes. It is a curiously uncontrolled, self-revealing laugh, for a man of Freddie Vigar's background to laugh at a man of Howard's. Howard is very touched by it. He laughs, too, putting his head back and looking at the ceiling. Really, this is just about the most entertaining and agreeable conversation he has ever taken part in!

'Missed you on television,' says Freddie. 'Been following your letters to the editor, though. Great interest. What are you working on at the moment?'

Howard explains, hesitatingly, about how he is trying to establish contact, through parties like this, with as wide a cross-section as possible of people who sort of share his views about the world, and to act as a sort of focus of dissent, and as a sort of clearing-house for sort of new ideas. He is afraid that to Freddie it will all sound naïvely idealistic, and rather nebulous. But not at all. Freddie tilts his head sympathetically and nods sideways at everything.

'This is immensely interesting,' he murmurs from time to time. 'Fearfully intriguing. Feel colossally guilty I haven't done anything like it myself.'

He is so interested in Howard's doings that Howard almost forgets to return the compliment.

'I'm sorry,' he says belatedly. 'Boring on like this about myself. What are *you* doing these days?'

But Freddie reacts oddly to this question. He looks away and takes another dry biscuit.

'Oh,' he says. 'Me. Well. You haven't heard?'

'No?' says Howard.

'Well,' says Freddie, not meeting Howard's eye. 'I'm afraid I'm God.'

'I beg your pardon?' says Howard.

Freddie clears his throat, and forces himself to look Howard in the eye.

'I said, I'm God.'

He folds his arms very tightly, and looks away over Howard's shoulder. He is plainly embarrassed. So is Howard. He is embarrassed to have embarrassed Freddie.

'I'm terribly sorry,' says Howard.

'Can't be helped,' says Freddie. 'Just one of those things.'

'I mean, I'm sorry not to have known.'

'Not at all. I'm sorry I had to spring it on you like that.'

There is an awkward silence. Freddie fiddles with his dry biscuit, breaking it into small pieces, and dropping crumbs which catch in the hairy surface of his trousers.

'Well,' says Howard. 'Congratulations.'

'Oh,' says Freddie. 'Thanks.'

The more Howard thinks about it, the less he knows where to look or what to do with his hands. He tries putting them behind his back and looking at the floor, smiling reflectively. Freddie is having difficulties, too. He puts his dry biscuit down, and with his left hand seizes his right elbow. With his right hand he takes hold of his chin. Then he, too, examines the floor.

'On second thoughts,' he says, 'I don't know about congratulations. Not like being elected to a fellowship, or whatever. Wasn't open to other candidates, you see.'

'Of course not,' says Howard.

'Bit difficult to put the thing into words, really. One is who one is. That's about it, I suppose.'

'But that's what counts, isn't it? Being who one is. One is who one is, so one does what one does.'

Freddie sighs.

'Not a great deal one *can* do,' he says, 'if one is who one is in this particular case.'

Howard raises his eyebrows.

'Surely . . .' he says.

'No, no,' says Freddie. 'One can't go writing letters to the papers, like you. The more one can do, the more careful one has to be not to go and do it. One has to think twice before one orders a cup of coffee, in case one's making use of one's position. One ends up pretty much as a signature on cheques.'

'But . . .' says Howard.

'To get anything done at all,' says Freddie, 'one has to move in tremendously mysterious ways. Terrifically glad if you could bear to look in for a drink the next time you're in town. See if we could combine forces.'

It's funny to be driving up to town again. Howard is wearing a very pale grey suit, with a pale blue shirt and a white silk tie, to set off the suntan he has acquired in the country. As he approaches the city on the freeway the same old restless excitement stirs in him that he felt on that first apocalyptic evening all those years ago. Under the clear summer morning sky the traffic thickens. All around him other men in pale suits are driving into town. Their shirts are crisp, their chins smooth, their cuffs stretch beyond their sleeves and rest lightly on their gold watch bracelets. They are self-contained, metropolitan, moving calmly towards their metropolitan importance.

And outwardly he is exactly like them.

Only browner.

There's the Pan-Am sign. And *Dagens Nyheter*. There's a new one, too, advertising Stella Artois. Things are changing.

And there, suddenly, as the expressway turns to cross wharves and black industrial water, are the towers of the inner city, grey-blue against the white-blue of the lower sky; authoritative and heart-stopping, in spite of everything.

The temperature is seventy-seven, the humidity in the low thirties. The stock market is rising.

And here he is, returning in triumph from his exile, for drinks with God, no less!

He walks round the streets he walked round on that first morning. Here's the café where he sat down and read all the papers, trying to understand the local politics. Here's the shopping street he walked along, and, lingering in it like the smell of coffee, the first impression of the whole city that he based on it.

Here's the flight of steps and the balustrade where he first set eyes on Rose.

A bus passes with a familiar number. On an impulse he runs after it and jumps aboard. It climbs steeply through trees, into quiet hillside streets from which little lanes and stairways drop suddenly down into the blue distances of the city. By the Congregational Church he gets off, and walks along the small gravelled cul-de-sac to their old house.

It's much smaller than he remembered it. He always thought of it as some kind of converted dungeon, but he sees now, with a wry smile, that it's really just an ordinary suburban house. Through the living-room window he can see a playpen, and a child's pot standing on the table.

The creosoted gate leading to the sideway and the back parts of the house judders open, sticking in its frame, and a youngish man emerges. He is slightly overweight, with a high, balding forehead, and dry hair that floats in the wind.

'Can I help you at all?' he asks Howard politely.

'Sorry,' says Howard. 'I was just looking at the place. I used to live here.'

'Really? Well, come in. Take a proper look.'

And he very kindly shows Howard all over the house and garden.

'We love it,' says the man. 'We were very lucky to find it, as a matter of fact. The children can walk to school without crossing a road anywhere. And it's a rather good school. Quite high academic standards – but with a reasonable social mix.'

Howard had vaguely remembered a whole series of gardens and courtyards, overhanging the city below. He almost laughs when he sees what it really is – a small lawn, with a rockery and kitchen garden beyond. You can only get the famous view of the city by standing on the compost-heap against the fence at the bottom.

He can't help being rather touched by the young man's enthusiasm about it all. Howard rather takes to him. He's got the kind of seriousness which he admires and a certain way of leaning forward as he shows Howard round, as if he is eager to understand the world but finds it rather difficult.

'It's quite handy for my work, too. I'm in mountains. I don't know whether you've seen anything in the paper about a mountain called the Matterhorn . . . ?'

Howard turns and looks at him sharply. Of course! It's himself, ten years younger.

Howard is relieved and pleased that his younger self could pass such a test; to have been in his own company for fifteen minutes or more, and to have been so opaque and convincing that he'd seemed to be like anyone else. He examines the young man curiously. Now that he knows it's himself he can't help noticing the slightly ridiculous and embarrassing qualities – the way the young man frowns importantly as he talks about his job, and waves his arms about when he gets stuck for words; and the way he smiles insincerely at Howard from time to time, and looks straight into his eyes in an effort to demonstrate that he is interested in Howard as well as himself. But since he never even notices that Howard *is* himself Howard takes this with a pinch of salt.

In the end Howard tells him. The young man stares at him, appalled.

'Don't worry,' says Howard, grinning. 'You're doing fine. I'm really quite pleased. You keep on like this, and one day you may find yourself in my position.'

The young man recollects himself, and manages a polite smile.

'Oh good,' he says. 'I look forward to that.'

Howard almost laughs aloud at the young man's distaste for the prospect. He has found out one thing in the ten years that separate them, if nothing else; that now is always better than then.

———

Caroline, Freddie's wife, looks rather like him, except that whereas Freddie's smile disappears up round the righthand side of his face, hers goes up to the left. So that when they sit facing each other on either side of their fireplace, both grins take off in the direction of the mantelpiece, as if drawn by the draught.

Howard sits on the long sofa between them, facing the Rembrandt. The ancient silk upholstery of the sofa is touchingly faded and threadbare. The carpet has obviously been in the family for years, too, and the Rembrandt is unrestored and almost completely black.

Howard sips his sherry, and tries not to wave his arms about as he explains how they converted their house.

'Yur,' says Freddie at intervals. He is wearing another crumpled three-piece suit, and another tie which sags to reveal his brass collar-stud.

'Yur,' adds Caroline sympathetically. She is a kindly-looking girl with thick white legs, and her slip showing.

They have seven children. Some of them are away at school, some being looked after by Nanny, in the upper parts of the house.

The house is in the centre of the city, on the edge of the Park, two minutes' walk from the best shops and the square where all the dropouts and drug-addicts meet. Through the windows you should have a good view of the RCA tower and the Hilton hotel. But the bottom of all the surrounding buildings is hidden by the high brick wall round the garden, and the top of them by the beige silk shades which are half-lowered over the windows. Everything inside the house is beige or dark brown or faded pastel; good but slightly worn; human but impersonal.

Howard sits back a little on the sofa. He feels very much at home.

'I suppose in a way I always really knew it was you,' he says. 'From that first time I met you. Because as soon as one starts to think about it seriously it's obvious. It *has* to be you. There's no one else who would even begin to be plausible.'

'Terrifically kind,' says Freddie, putting his head on one side and grinning awkwardly. 'No special skill involved, though. Anyone could do it.'

'Oh, come, come!' smiles Howard.

'No, really . . .'

'Howard's right, darling,' murmurs Caroline. 'You mustn't keep running yourself down. It's a dreadful bore for all the rest of us.'

'Oh, dear,' says Freddie, knotting his arms and legs together in embarrassment.

'I can't help feeling,' says Howard, sticking his head forward ruefully, 'now I know who you are, that I've been a bit outspoken in some of my remarks about the system.'

'Not at all!' says Freddie.

'Not a bit!' says Caroline.

'But I must in all honesty say,' says Howard very quickly, jutting his chin out and smilingly blinking his eyes, 'that I still think there are a number of things in the universe which really need seriously looking into.'

'Oh, the whole thing!' says Freddie with feeling.

'Ghastly mess,' says Caroline.

'Absolute disaster area,' says Freddie.

'Frightful,' says Caroline.

'So far as one can understand it,' says Freddie.

'Freddie feels frightfully strongly about it, you see,' says Caroline.

Howard looks from one to the other in astonishment.

'Good heavens!' he says. 'I should never have guessed . . .'

'Oh, Freddie's a terrific radical,' says Caroline.

'*Really?*' says Howard.

'A terrible firebrand, really,' says Caroline.

Freddie knots himself up.

'A bit firebrandish,' he admits.

'A bit of a Maoist, to tell you the truth,' says Caroline. She looks sideways at Howard to see how he is taking this. So does Freddie.

'A *Maoist?*' says Howard, astonished.

'Permanent revolution,' says Caroline.

'That style of thing,' agrees Freddie.

'What he feels, you see,' says Caroline, 'is that people ought to struggle pretty well all the time against the limitations of the world and their own nature. Not stop.'

Howard gazes at Freddie, deeply impressed.

'Don't worry,' says Freddie. 'I don't think my views have much effect.'

'Don't be silly,' says Caroline. 'People have a lot of respect for them.'

'I'm not sure they even notice them.'

'*I* notice them,' says Howard fervently. '*I* respect them.'

'You see?' says Caroline.

'Rather cheering meeting you, I must admit,' says Freddie. 'Fearfully difficult in this job to know if one's having much effect on things. One tries to – well – set a bit of an example. If that's not too sanctimonious!'

'Not at all!' cries Howard. 'Thank God someone is still prepared to make a moral stand like this!'

'I told you, darling,' says Caroline.

'Sometimes,' says Freddie, 'one's tempted to just plunge in and put everything to rights.'

'I know the feeling,' says Howard warmly.

'But if one really believes in participatory democracy, and all that kind of thing, one has to be a bit constitutional about it.'

'Of course,' says Howard.

'Paradoxically.'

'You do jog things along a bit behind the scenes, though, darling,' says Caroline. 'You do drop a hint here and there.'

'That's the most one can do, really,' says Freddie. 'Get hold of some ordinary chap and drop a few hints in his ear.'

'That's why Freddie asked you to come round today,' says Caroline.

'Perhaps "ordinary chap" is a rather unfortunate phrase . . .'

'Not at all,' says Howard. 'You couldn't find a more ordinary chap than me.'

'What I thought,' says Freddie, 'was that we could fix you up with some kind of nominal job in the organization . . .'

'Like Managing Director,' says Caroline.

'Or Prime Minister,' says Freddie. 'Something like that. Then between us possibly we could begin to stir things up a bit.'

Howard frowns at his glass, trying to conceal his pleasure.

'Well,' he says.

'I haven't put it very well,' says Freddie, screwing his head round sideways.

'The ideas would be yours as much as Freddie's,' says Caroline.

'I'd just make the odd suggestion from time to time,' says Freddie.

'Well,' says Howard. His hands are shaking slightly.

'It's not the kind of thing that would influence you, of course,' says Caroline, 'but the prospects would be quite good.'

'Because I don't suppose I shall go on forever,' smiles Freddie. 'Anyway, perhaps you'd think it over.'

'Yur,' says Howard thoughtfully, putting his head on one side. 'Yur.'

Howard and Felicity don't go mad. They don't let the new job make any great difference to their lives. They have to buy a house in town, of course, so that Howard can be near his work during the week. It's two minutes' walk across the Park from the sombre baronial building where he has his office; there's no point in not living centrally now the children are away at school. But otherwise it's quite modest. A little walled garden, with a few pollarded lime trees in it, and one or two urns and busts, and a solitary policeman tucked away in a little sentry-box inside the gateway. Inside the house the furniture and the pictures on the walls are all dark brown. Everything is old, and well-polished, and slightly worn. It's not some brash statement of their own personalities, but a low murmur from many people over many years.

Howard and Felicity sit facing each other in the evenings across the empty fireplace (they have central heating, of course, and there's no point in getting soot in the curtains unless they have guests). He wears a dark three-piece suit, but from a sense of natural modesty he has his suits considerably better cut than Freddie's. Felicity wears a beige twin set, but keeps her slip modestly out of sight.

'It feels better, doesn't it?' says Howard. 'If one's honest with oneself.'

'I've always preferred old things and quiet colours,' says Felicity. 'In myself – underneath.'

Howard draws on his pipe. (He smokes a pipe now.)

'When one's first married,' he says, 'when one's first down from university, one keeps striking attitudes. One's whole style of life is intended to make claims about oneself – to announce one's group-loyalties and relationship with the world. The rest of one's life is a process of dropping the claims, one by one. And with each claim one drops, one feels better. More relaxed. More honest. More *oneself*. The less one makes of oneself, the more one *is* oneself. The less one is who one thinks one ought to be, the more one is who one is. I feel more myself now than ever.'

'Yur,' says Felicity. 'Terrifically true.'

They *all* live in solid old houses near the Park now – the Chases, the Bernsteins, the Waylands, Charles Aught, the Goodys – their whole set. They all have dark brown pictures on their walls, and oatmeal skirts, and umber dogs. The only thing the rest of them lack is a policeman at the gate.

'We really do seem to have taken over,' says Prue at her dinner-parties, looking at them all.

'There has been a real revolution, when you think about it,' says Michael Wayland.

'A kind of quiet revolution, from within,' says Miriam Bernstein.

'The only sort that works,' says Charles Aught.

'Oh, there's no doubt about it,' says Bill Goody. 'There's been a radical change in the whole structure of society during the last few years.'

So radical has the change been that Freddie and Caroline are sometimes at Prue's dinner-parties now. Which is agreeable. Although in some ways it's even more agreeable when they're not, because then Howard does his famous imitation of Freddie – Freddie being praised, Freddie being jealous, Freddie doing his best to unbend enough to be wrathful. Howard has got him beautifully.

'*Dear* Howard,' murmurs Prue, pressing his hand. She never forgets that it's Howard to whom they all owe their place in the new order of things.

The only people who seem to have failed to benefit from the revolution are Phil and Rose. They are living in some slightly embarrassing suburb – the kind of suburb that has a dog track, and an immigrant problem.

Phil rather faded out after his terrible fiasco with the première of Man. Months and months of advance publicity, and newspaper articles about the seriousness and dedication of everyone involved – then the curtains parted, and out on to the stage walked a rather tubby little figure with a balding forehead and thin hair flying in the wind, who leaned anxiously forward and waved his arms about as he talked. The audience began to trickle away as he told a series of long, rambling stories to which he forgot the punchlines, conducted a hesitant affair with somebody else's wife, and announced half-baked plans for an ideal world. The reviews next morning were disastrous. 'This self-important manikin simply will not do . . . a unique combination of vanity, greed, and incompetence . . . his capacity for deceiving himself about his own motives would seem boundless . . . under-developed arm and shoulder muscles . . . a chronic inability to formulate sublime thoughts . . . if the production models are not a vast improvement on this pitiful prototype, God help us all . . .'

'Poor old Phil,' Howard says to Felicity at quite frequent intervals. 'I suppose he always was too clever by half. All the same, I can't help feeling rather sorry for him. And for Rose. I suppose she married him with her eyes open. Still . . .'

'We must have them to dinner some time,' says Felicity.

'Who with, though? That's the problem.'

They think hard, but as Freddie says, you can't just plunge in unilaterally and put everything to rights.

'Poor Phil,' says Felicity.

'Poor Rose,' says Howard.

At the office Howard surrounds himself with a team of young men and women just down from university. They are all newly married, with small babies who are allowed to stay up to dinner to talk amusingly about sex. They wear brightly coloured shirts, and their hair falls in front of their eyes as they talk.

Howard is very fond of them all. They are his creations – he has chosen them himself, and provided each one with a livelihood and a way of being. And they amuse him. He is tickled by the idea they all have of him as a fool and a hypocrite and a mass-murderer. He plays up to them, producing shocking ideas and attitudes which he lets himself half-believe. They know that he is playing a part; they are amused by his attempts to amuse them; and grow fond of him; and thereby demonstrate their own tolerance to themselves; and grow even fonder of him as the occasion of the demonstration. He enjoys their affection. And what he enjoys even more is the knowledge that their affection is based upon patronizing him from what they take to be their greater radicalism; while in fact, under the surface, he is more radical than they will ever be. He feels the piquant double pleasure of the secret millionaire who has won everyone's heart even in apparent poverty.

The radicalism of the young people in his office consists in this: that they want to create an ideal world flowing with milk and honey, where man is brother to man, and lives in harmony with nature; where ice is warm to the touch, and no ocean is too wide for a child to wade across, bucket and spade in hand.

But he can see, from the vantage-point of his experience of life, how shallow and patronizing this conception of happiness is. *His* radicalism now takes this form (and Freddie is in more or less complete agreement): to help all men enjoy the same possibilities for happiness as he does himself – no less.

And what has made his own life in this society so deeply pleasurable (as he now sees, looking back on it) is the *difficulty* of it, the opportunity it has offered to strive and overcome. He has had to struggle with nature; compete with the most brilliant men and women of his generation; labour to outstrip his own achievements. His life here has been one long series of decisions taken with difficulty, of crises resolved. And in the process he has developed and grown: His intelligence and sensibility and compassion have been stretched.

His life has a sense of purposive onward movement. This is the heart of the matter.

So the universe he is trying to build is one which offers its inhabitants the possibility of moral action; one which challenges its inhabitants to transcend it.

He discreetly steers the old Alps plan through, and fosters ambitious projects to stud shipping routes with underwater rocks, and the atmosphere with unpredictable patterns of clear-air turbulence. He throws his weight behind the creation of a vast sub-arctic tundra, where labour camps could be built and great writers developed. He's also intrigued by a proposal for a desert with just enough vegetation to support a group of nomadic tribes, and exactly the right mix of privation to enable these tribes to develop a monotheistic religion. Monotheism could be a very suggestive metaphor, he feels.

'Because what we're aiming at,' he philosophizes to his young graduates, when he invites them round to dinner, in twos and threes, together with the Chases or the Waylands, and sometimes Freddie and Caroline, 'is something deeper than a little physical hardship. What we have to build is a universe so manifestly and intrinsically unjust that its inhabitants cannot fail to rebel against it. Permanent revolution – this is the only interesting human condition. Only in rejecting the terms on which life is offered to him can a man discover his real dignity, his real self.'

The young graduates lift the hair out of their eyes, and for an instant glance round the room at the rather good, slightly worn furnishings. Then they look at each other and quickly look away again, trying not to smile.

'That's why,' says Howard, 'we must make sure that the terms they are offered are self-evidently unacceptable . . . Another slice of lamb, anyone? More beans . . . ? Because the greatness of man is to see that things might be otherwise – to look at the world around him, and to see another world beneath its surface.'

He stands there, carving knife and fork poised over the remains of the *gigot aux haricots*, and looks inquiringly round the table at the brightly coloured shirts and three-piece suits, and sees, beneath the surface, emaciated men in rags and foot-clouts, holding out tin bowls for a little soup, their eyes reflecting the freezing emptiness of the tundra.

'This is our task,' he says, emphasizing each phrase with a wave of the carving knife; 'to provide the harsh materials on which men's imaginations can be exercised, and to offer, through the cultured and civilized life that we ourselves lead here in the metropolis, some intimation of the world they might envisage.'

'Meanwhile,' murmurs Miriam Bernstein, 'here we all sit waiting for second helpings.'

And even now that he has achieved all this he doesn't stand still. He continues to grow.

Day by day he develops and becomes yet more mature.

His understanding of the world continues to deepen. So does his understanding of himself.

His relationship with the universe becomes more subtle and devious.

Things couldn't be better. Because every day they *are*.

So when one fine morning he comes into his inner office and his principal private secretary says that Phil Schaffer has phoned, he stops in his tracks, grinning. The idea of going out to the suburb with the dog track, and confronting the confusions and embarrassments of his past life with the formidable armoury of maturity and understanding that he now possesses, appears suddenly very sweet. For there is one small drawback to things getting better and better all the time. The better they get, the better and better they could have been; and no one likes to leave a past behind him that could have been better.

'I'll be back some time this afternoon,' he tells his principal private secretary.

'But what about your lunch with the Japanese Prime Minister?' cries his principal private secretary. 'What about your State of the Nation speech?'

But Howard only laughs.

He takes one of the smaller cars and drives himself. He doesn't want to put on any show. It's going to be difficult enough offering Phil some kind of job without causing offence.

As he waits at a stop-light somewhere out beyond the freight-yards he drums his fingers on the steering wheel and gazes straight in front of him, thinking. He is wondering:

— whether he is on the right road or not;

— whether he should kiss Rose when he arrives;

— whether he will be invited to lunch, and if not, whether he should get a sandwich in a pub instead, and if so, whether he would prefer egg and tomato, or cheese and chutney;

— whether the girl standing on the opposite side of the crossroads, with her face hidden by the long dark hair falling over her shoulders as she waits to cross the road, head turned to watch the oncoming traffic, will look straight ahead so that he can see her face; and if so, whether it will fulfil his hopes; and whether the fulfilment of his hopes would in itself be a kind of disappointment.

The traffic-light, which has been green for some time, turns red.

The girl crosses. She does fulfil his hopes, in a way; and the fulfilment of them is in itself a kind of disappointment; and her name is Rose.

'Rose!' he calls, and prinks on the hooter. She turns to look at him in surprise. Grinning and waving, he puts the car into gear and steps on the accelerator. He will zoom up to her, stop with a screech of brakes, and ask her something like when lighting-up time is. She will be half pleased to see him and half disapproving; and that will be the beginning once again of something so painful and awkward that the possibility of happiness must be concealed in it somewhere.

But when he gets to the other side of the crossroads it's not Rose, after all. It's a revolving figure, a hundred feet tall, advertising cigarettes. Beyond her, further along the expressway, are flashing signs bearing the symbols of the Chrysler Corporation and Asahi Pentax.

Of course! At sunset, with the sky red and the road wet after a day of storms, he is approaching some great metropolis. A restless excitement stirs in him, a sense of being on the verge of deep and different things . . .

Anthony Powell

A Dance to the Music of Time

'The most significant work of fiction produced in England since the last war.' *Clive James*

FLAMINGO

Recent novels by
Beryl Bainbridge

Watson's Apology

'Mysterious and compelling . . . a remarkable book.'
Anita Brookner, *Standard*

Young Adolf

'A delightful fantasy . . . the adventures of the malnourished
16-year-old are recounted with Chaplinesque glee.' *Listener*

Winter Garden

'Razor sharp, most appealing . . . a graceful, disturbing
thriller.' *New York Times Book Review*

and

Injury Time
The Dressmaker
Harriet Said . . .
The Bottle Factory Outing

FLAMINGO

FLAMINGO

Flamingo is a quality imprint publishing both fiction and non-fiction. Below are some recent titles.

Fiction
- [ ] The Laughter of Carthage *Michael Moorcock* £4.50
- [ ] Foggage *Patrick McGinley* £2.95
- [ ] The Wall of the Plague *André Brink* £3.95
- [ ] Watson's Apology *Beryl Bainbridge* £2.95
- [ ] Les Belles Images *Simone de Beauvoir* £2.50
- [ ] The Burden *Vladimir Rybakov* £2.95
- [ ] The Railway Station Man *Jennifer Johnston* £2.95
- [ ] The Siege of Krishnapur *J. G. Farrell* £3.50

Non-fiction
- [ ] Scottish Journey *Edwin Muir* £3.50
- [ ] The Perfect Stranger *P. J. Kavanagh* £2.50
- [ ] Order Out of Chaos *Ilya Prigogine* £3.95
- [ ] My Last Breath *Luis Buñuel* £3.50
- [ ] Mind and Nature *Gregory Bateson* £3.50
- [ ] English Journey *Beryl Bainbridge* £2.50
- [ ] Thinking About Thinking *Antony Flew* £2.50
- [ ] Manners from Heaven *Quentin Crisp* £2.50

You can buy Flamingo paperbacks at your local bookshop or newsagent. Or you can order them from Fontana Paperbacks, Cash Sales Department, Box 29, Douglas, Isle of Man. Please send a cheque, postal or money order (not currency) worth the purchase price plus 15p per book (maximum postal charge is £3.00 for orders within the UK).

NAME (Block letters) _____

ADDRESS_____

_____

_____